A YEAR IN PARADISE

A Year in Paradise

Published by T.A.C. Press
Copyright © Barbara Lewis, 2018

ISBN: 9781911047605

Designed by Monica Franco
www.printtailors.com

A YEAR IN
PARADISE

Barbara Lewis

TAC
LONDON

SUMMER

1

It's August 15th, the dead centre of summer, when nominally Catholic Europe marks lazily the Feast of the Assumption, when heaven received Mary's miraculously uncorrupted body. And it's the middle of the afternoon. The sun blazes down on vines loaded with grapes. It should be a vintage year, although the *Cognacais* like to say that every year is a vintage year. Cognac, at its best, they say, is a glorious blend, a triumph over time contrived by the *maître-de-chai*, or master blender. Year-in, year-out, he creates the same even harmony however unpromising the raw *eaux-de-vie*.

The grapes hang translucent and motionless, sweetening in the suffocating heat. All of nature is still. The only rash movement is a cyclist. Clad in Lycra, dripping with sweat, he defies his environment, forcing his pace, scorching along the dusty limestone road, barely more than a path. He is going nowhere in particular, just desperate to be on the move. In so far as he's thinking, he's imagining what life might be if he were a champion cyclist in the Tour de France, speeding his way through kilometre after kilometre of French countryside, and he is pushing to the back of his mind the nagging sensation that he is slightly bored or is it dissatisfied or both? Are they not nearly always one and the same? As an adult, every deed he has ever done has been at worst harmful and at best pointless, but then he would argue that ultimately everything is pointless, so what does it matter? What does it matter to anyone but himself that in a random universe he is rich, mostly because he was born rich and advantaged and makes money by making others poorer? On he speeds, restlessly wondering if the nagging, almost panic-stricken sensation of absence is because he misses the adrenaline of doing a deal with a distressed seller and selling minutes later to someone desperate to buy and, in the process, raising the price for everyone else. He's almost ready to get off his bike and make a few calls from the limited shade the vines throw even in their full summer leafiness, when through his sweat-drenched eyelashes, he sees the first car he has seen in hours and like almost everything else, it is utterly still. It has swerved to a halt with extreme finality, a front wheel at an awkward angle in the edge of the vineyard and the rest of the vehicle blocking the narrow route. His first thought is irritation, his reaction to any obstacle. Obliged to dismount, he approaches impatiently and notices fragments of glass glinting in the sunlight. The windows are riddled with bullet holes and this is no ordinary car. It's a limousine with a driver in a uniform, slumped over the steering wheel. Behind him are a man and a woman. The man, strangely familiar, is wearing a white Arabian *thawb* vivid with blood. The woman has a bullet wound in her forehead. She is wearing an *abaya* whose inky black hood has fallen askew as her head jerked back. Paul scans the area. Whoever did this has fled, without a trace, without a witness. Uncharacteristically, Paul Gray is paralysed, indecisive. In this suddenly very foreign-feeling country, he doesn't even know how to call the police. Shaking slightly as the sweat begins to cool and a chill shudders through him, he is contemplating just cycling off, back the way he came, and pretending he has seen nothing when Bénédicte Rivet gallops up through the vines on her horse Oscar. Oscar is the colour of dark honey, you could even say cognac, and slim enough to be comfortable for Bénédicte, *une petite Cognacaise*. She dismounts, absentmindedly patting Oscar as her wide brown eyes widen in horror and Paul musters in faltering French: *"Il faut appeler la police."* Bénédicte does not reply immediately, then in English, with a strong French accent, she says: "Listen." Paul's strongest emotion is to feel insulted that his French was not sufficiently authentic to be answered in French. "Listen," she says again, oblivious to his wounded pride, and he hears a murmur and now she is tugging at the car door. "Someone is alive." Passively, he looks on as the door swings open, sending a cascade of glass on to the roadside and a child crawls out, whimpering, from beneath her dead mother's skirts. *"Mon dieu,"* Bénédicte exclaims and scoops the child, a girl, maybe two or three years old, into her arms. "We have to call the police," Paul pleads, handing Bénédicte his precious, state-of-the-art phone, full of numbers of useful, monied people. She hands him the child, then makes an emergency call to tell a half-asleep policeman something atrocious has happened in *la Grande Champagne.*

2

Paul cycles over the rough, chalky drive bordered by linden trees that leads to his home - if that's what it is. It's a seventeenth century limestone house he bought on a whim after an averagely profitable trading day. Rarely has he demonstrated such refined taste as in his delight for this perfectly symmetrical Cognacais house, with faded grey shutters and a low, red, tiled roof. He stows his obscenely expensive carbon-framed bike in one of his two barns. Reinforcing the symmetry of the main house, there is a barn on each side. One of them is a store for tools left by previous owners for growing vegetables and cultivating vines. They are long disused and yet ancient grey, dried-out mud still clings to the prongs of forks and adheres to rusting spades. The other houses a bulging copper *alembic*, once shining, now covered in cobwebs and verdigris.

Paul heaves shut the massive barn door and walks to open the central front door with its over-sized rusting key.

Even now at nine o'clock at night, the air outside is hot, but within the stone house, he feels as if he is drinking in a cool, soothing draught. He climbs the curving wooden staircase to take a shower in the big, Spartan bathroom and then, free of the dust of the day, he sinks into one of the leather armchairs placed either side of his dormant fireplace, a glass of cognac in hand. The police were laborious and unimaginative, fortunately for someone whose trading habits bear little scrutiny.

Paul's low, harmonious house is peasant-style compared with the lofty *maison bourgeoise* - Bénédicte's family home - that rises four storeys high above a double staircase up to the imposing front door. As Paul broods over his *digestif,* Bénédicte is in the stables washing down Oscar. She is thorough and patient as she is in almost everything she does, except her pace is slowed even more than usual by her desire to stay within the refuge of this moment. It's a moment of profound continuity, tinged with the painful awareness of its fragility. Since her early teenage years, she has hidden herself away in these stables, first with Ombre, who is no more, and now with Oscar. She has no desire to return to the empty flat she rents in Cognac or to enter the family home where her father worries about the price of *eaux-de-vie*, distilled from his vines in Cognac's finest growing area, which he will sell to Cauvet, the grandest, but not necessarily most generous of the cognac houses, and her mother frets over her sister, Dominique, who yet again is entangled with the wrong man. This time it's serious. She is deeply in love, she says, with a man she has only just met and her parents consider to be little better than a tramp. For Dominique, he is a hero, standing up to empty convention and corrupt vested interest. Together they plan to set up an alternative community in the Gironde to spread their political vision among paying guests, but first, they need to persuade *Monsieur et Madame* Rivet to invest in the project. Bénédicte is firmly on her parents' side. At best, she thinks Dominique's *amour* is an obsessive bore, thrusting his views on all around, and at worst a parasite, but she says nothing of that to Dominique. Dominique never listens to her in any case. She is just the hopelessly straight-laced elder sister who can't even snare the man she has been sighing over for months. Dominique, on the other hand, has systematically dictated the atmosphere of the household and commanded all her mother's emotional energy since her birth. The responsible elder sister is left feeling duty-bound to absorb quietly whatever strange emotions she has experienced today or any other day and carry on not exactly as normal, but exactly as before.

It would only add to the strangeness for Bénédicte to learn that Oscar is not the only equestrian connection to

the bodies in the car and that Cognac's police Commander
Frédéric de Massol is puzzling over that fact as he sits
before his grey, metal desk in the dowdy Cognac police
building, tucked away at the railway station end of town.
His emotions are mixed in so far as they are emotions. He
is bitter and self-righteous that the team that resentfully
serves him has long gone home, leaving him to work alone
on the report that must be filed to Paris. His colleagues,
relatively speaking, have rich, fulfilled lives. He has merely
a modest career as the head of a provincial outpost.
Girlfriend after girlfriend has melted away. And anything
he ever felt for them was nothing compared with the
feverish excitement tingling through his veins. He believes
his career will never be the same but is not arrogant
enough to be unaware that the line between glory and
abject failure has rarely been finer. The bodies in the car
were the bodies of the world's most powerful oil minister
and his wife, together with a chauffeur from the Cauvet
cognac house, who had been driving them to the air base to
board their private jet home. A day before, they had been
the distinguished guests of the Cauvet family, dining in the
family *château* with a select circle including the *maître-de-
chai*, and the day before that they had been to the coast to
see the stables of the Cauvet family horses, some of them
Arabian thoroughbreds sold to the Cauvets by the oil
minister's illustrious connections. The trip to Cognac was
all about nurturing such ties with both sides motivated

by the expectation they could somehow be useful to one another. The Cauvets saw potential sales in the supposedly alcohol-averse Middle East. The oil minister was seduced by status, luxury and good breeding, as is de Massol. De Massol's main problem is not that his origins are ordinary, but that he aspires with every fibre in his lean frame to be part of an élite. His serving officers whisper that he bought the *"de"* of his surname in a desperate attempt to be aristocratic. For that they despise him. Someone proud to have succeeded on his own merits, they could respect.

3

Cold in a morgue, twenty-four hours earlier, oil minister Zak al-Asad had feasted on the finest life could offer in the Cauvet *château*. And he hadn't enjoyed it. The chandeliers twinkled, the silver cutlery sparkled, course after exquisite course appeared before him and, barely touched, was discreetly removed by white-gloved hands. After dinner, the assembled guests, the minister included, drifted on to the terrace to sip their glasses of extremely complex, long-aged cognac, rich with tannin and vanilla. Only al-Asad's wife excused herself to slip away to the guest bedroom graciously loaned for the night, with its plump pillows and heavy, festooned curtains, and reassure herself of the safety of her sleeping daughter. Had she lived, the mother would in future years have cherished the deep luxury of that hushed hour of bonding away from the strain of conversation whose superficial meaning belied a deeper intrigue. She knew her husband was relieved that she had left him to whatever business he was conducting. She suspected some desperate scheme to cling to office, while basking in the hospitality designed to reassure him of his continued importance, when he knew that she knew he could never have had time for a trip like this at the height of his power. Neither would he have allowed his wife to accompany him. He rarely took her anywhere. She guessed it was only his newfound insecurity that made him hold on to his wife and daughter as a child clutches at a toy.

On the terrace, al-Asad is next to *maître-de-chai* Gilles Castaniet, who is explaining wearily the significance of blending *eaux-de-vie*. Some cognac houses believe in selling single vintages. They appeal, for instance, to the U.S. market, he says, exuding French disdain, where millionaires like to pour cognac of the year of their birth in the ridiculous assumption they are as significant as the spirit they drink. Cauvet sticks by its blends. There is of course a commercial logic. Some years are better than others. Blending allows the unevenness of nature to be ironed out and preserves the correct balance of the stocks of *eaux-de-vie*, stored in carefully-guarded warehouses, known as *chais*, on the banks of the River Charente. Still, the Cauvet house and the Castaniet family, which for generations has provided chief tasters – or *maîtres-de-chai* – for the Cauvets, pride themselves on their superior blending skills.

The minister listens thoughtfully. He is as proud of the high-quality, low-sulphur crude oil his country exports as Cauvet is of its meticulously blended cognac and he understands it as intimately. An oil man through and through, he trained as a geologist and worked his way up the ranks, right to the top despite his humble birth. Until very recently, he was confident of his own merit. To the outside world, he still appears unassailably in charge, but he knows enemies are gathering in the corridors, outside his door, blaming him for the falling oil price, whispering in corners that he has lost his touch. In Castaniet, he sees someone else who has devoted his life to a product that fashionable opinion says does more harm than good, but Castaniet has yet to acknowledge he is becoming an anachronism.

"How do they decide on the price of the *eau-de-vie*?" al-Asad suddenly asks.

Castaniet smiles a knowing French smile.

"It's a long story," he says.

"But is there an open market or do the producers get together and agree?"

"It's actually the buyers who agree," Castaniet says after a long pause, not convinced he should be revealing so much of a practice officially denied because it infuriates the *viticulteurs*.

"Shouldn't it be the other way round?" al-Asad naturally responds.

"Not if you're the buyer," says Castaniet.

"And you're not worried the producers will organise themselves?"

"Well, we own some of them and for the others it's still an honour to supply to us as a luxury house." Castaniet doesn't say that the world's most powerful oil minister is dealing in a mere commodity, subject to the winds of recession and supply and demand, but the put-down is felt. Al-Asad nods very slightly and shifts away to stare out into the well-groomed grounds. Lawns gently rolling down to an artificial lake look matt in the moonlight. He wonders if he would have made it to the top if he had been born in *la France profonde*, and if he had, whether the sense of failure would be the same. You rise so far and then realise as you look out from the summit, the only way for you is down and it's someone else's turn to ascend. The pointlessness overwhelms and the will for the relentless struggle to hold on to status or even life itself ebbs away.

4

Bénédicte is sitting in her office at Cognac Cauvet. The building is largely deserted as anyone with a family has disappeared for the rest of the month, including the department secretary Véronique, who shares the office with Bénédicte. Bénédicte should be enjoying the peace, uninterrupted by endless phone calls and chatty secretaries bustling in for gossip, anathema to Bénédicte, who considers all that to be banal normality that leads nowhere. She had resolved to get so much work done over the summer lull. She has a writing project. It's the text for packaging for a new blend to mark the 150th anniversary of the first shipments to Asia. She had been thrilled to be included. Asia is *the* potential market for Cauvet. Cognac is a status symbol. Businessmen buy it to impress other businessmen. Families serve it to long-lost visitors at Chinese New Year or hand over bottles, gift-wrapped, as a good luck presents. Bénédicte has been spared the details, past and present, of any shady links to opium wars and nineteenth century triangular trade and of the beautiful young night club hostesses of today paid to dole out liberal doses to fat executives in private rooms. She is focused on the high romance of elegant clippers racing across the seas carrying cognac east and tea west. She writes down a few phrases in her note book – all the cognac in China; time – the most precious ingredient of Cauvet cognac – but nothing rings true. She's distracted. The image of those bodies and the traumatised toddler are indelible. The police told her to take time off to get over the shock, but she thought she'd rather work. Then there's that Englishman – a tall, dark stranger in Lycra. Bénédicte isn't sure he's her type and yet the otherness of his world has an allure and yet she is resolutely obsessed with Francois, one of Cauvet's hand-picked, fast-track trainee managers who manages exchange rate risks to prevent exposure to Asian currencies eating into the company profits. She picks up her phone and contemplates dialling his extension. She is pretty sure he is at his desk calculating how to augment Cauvet's handsome profits. She'd love to confide, but she knows from bitter experience he will snap at her that he is busy. Instead, she opens the window, admitting the heady smell of cognac, evaporating from the *chais*. They call the fumes the angels' share and it's especially intoxicating in the summer heat. On the quayside beside the river another boat-load of summer visitors clambers on to the Cauvetbranded ferry to cross to the other side and visit the rows upon rows of ageing *eaux-de-vie*. She can see the English guide Sophie is with them, immaculate in her uniform of crisp white dress and dark green blazer. In so far as Bénédicte hates any other human being, she hates Sophie. She hates the way she tosses her mane of blond wavy hair, so different from Bénédicte's utterly straight and merely dark brown hair. Bénédicte hates her bad French and ringing English accent and most of all she hates her power over Francois. She also hates herself for the adolescent, embarrassed emotions as *cherchez l'homme* dominates her thoughts and distracts her from any other ambition. She cannot imagine she will live to see a day when she could be nostalgic for this protracted green phase of her youth. She rails at Francois for putting cold career ambition first - that and dalliance with a here-today, gone-tomorrow summer guide.

She turns back to her office to see de Massol walk in. She is struck by his exaggerated height and his pinched thinness. Even in the summer heat, he looks cold. He is struck by the difference between Bénédicte's office and his own. The walls here are covered with soft-focus pictures of vines rolling down gentle slopes like the lines on candlewick bedspreads. Where he has sharp-edged metal cabinets, Bénédicte has heavy wooden shelves, stacked with a casual muddle of books and objects - a vase given by Chinese visitors and a wooden model of a bottle for the special blend of cognac whose launch she is working on.

"*Bonjour,*" he says and offers his hand stiffly. "I wanted to check you were okay." Civilities over, he has a few more questions. Had she ever met Paul Gray, the Englishman, before? No, she had not. Has she had any contact since? Again no, she has not.

"You give the impression you think he has something to do with it," she says, her wide eyes widening a little further. "I'm ruling nothing out or in," de Massol says primly.

Bénédicte thinks back to the scene. The Englishman had seemed so totally shocked. He couldn't have been acting. But then again, shock didn't rule out that he had just killed three people and thrown his gun far into the vines. But no, he wouldn't have been on a bicycle, surely and he wouldn't have hung around to wait for a passing stranger riding a horse and they would have found the gun by now.

After her thoughtful pause, Bénédicte asks about the little girl. "How is she?"

"It's hard to say," says de Massol. "She will not say a word in any language."

Bénédicte too is silenced, trying to imagine the horror, overwhelmed by a rush of gratitude for her own gentle parents.

De Massol moves on. He wants to be taken to Castaniet's office.

Bénédicte looks at her watch. It's 11.30. No-one ever disturbs Castaniet before noon. It's a cast-iron company rule. Between eight and noon every day Castaniet is locked in his tasting room alone, free from telephone calls and any other intrusion as he pursues the perfect blend.

She tells de Massol he must wait.

"When a murder has been committed, other rules must be broken," he grumbles.

"But surely there is someone else you could see first? The minister must have had a guide to show him round. Perhaps it's worth talking to the guides?" ventures Bénédicte.

Though it is far beneath his dignity to accept a suggestion, de Massol allows himself to be led off to the reception area where Sophie has just returned from the river crossing with her group of tourists and who should be among them but Paul.

"Hello" he says to both of them. "Thought I may as well do some sight-seeing to take my mind off things."

"Did it work?" de Massol asks dryly, self-conscious in English. In English, he can communicate, but less well when he finds his interlocutor unsympathetic. Any sense of weakness seems to be magnified and even though his English is undoubtedly better than Paul's French, he senses it allows Paul to reclaim his natural tendency to dominate, to seize the upper hand, a tendency instilled by expensive boarding school followed by unmitigated success provided you don't analyse his life career too deeply. De Massol's dislike of Paul is all the greater now that the initial shock has restored Paul's arrogant bearing. De Massol senses some sort of connection he can't put his finger on. He can just about believe that Bénédicte and Paul are virtual strangers, but what about the oil minister? Did he know him? He claims only that he knew of him, as did most of the adult population.

If only to give himself thinking time, de Massol turns his attention, as Bénédicte had suggested, to Sophie the guide, noticing out of the corner of his eye that Paul makes a beeline for Bénédicte. If they are strangers so far, he clearly wants to get better acquainted.

Sophie seems to him all innocence. She had indeed taken the oil minister to see *Le Paradis*. *Le Paradis*, she explains, quoting perfectly from the Cauvet guidebook, is where the most precious, oldest *eaux-de-vie* are stored under lock and key and in glass jars, not barrels because the ageing process is complete. They are stoppered up in glass, changing no more, until needed for the very best blends and they are valued so highly Cauvet has its very own fire brigade on standby, just in case.

"With all that wood and alcohol, a fire in the *chais* would be catastrophic," Sophie says earnestly.

"And how did the minister seem? Was he interested? Did he ask questions? What was his mood?" De Massol asks crisply, cutting into the tourist tour.

"He was very quiet. I'd say he had something on his mind," said Sophie. "But then I suppose important people often do have."

"Did he seem happy, unhappy, even frightened perhaps?"

"I wouldn't say happy, but I wouldn't say frightened either. Perhaps resigned."

De Massol puzzles over the word resigned - *resigné*? Is she implying she thought he expected to die?

"I can't know that from just showing him round," she laughs with a flash of perfect teeth. "I just meant he didn't have any *joie de vivre*. To be honest, I was disappointed how little interest he showed. It was *presque impoli*," she says, sprinkling in French to prove she can.

De Massol closes the interview, sensing he is getting nowhere. Bénédicte and Paul have melted away. Castaniet will have to wait. He has a press conference to organise.

5

Cognac's town hall, normally the seat of stubborn, slow-moving bureaucracy is buzzing with the anticipation of action. Television vans surround it and lengths of cable snake across the pavement. Within, in the room meant for civil marriages, de Massol sits at the top table flanked by a superior who has arrived from Paris and an interpreter to relay an English version. Uniformed officers line the walls, some are *gendarmes*, who almost had managed to claim jurisdiction over this rural murder, but de Massol has wrested control of his career-defining case as the victims had been staying in Cognac, which falls under the authority of the municipal police. The guests are the representatives of the press, tatty, permanently on deadline, and apparently unfeeling. They are from London, Paris, the Middle East and Cognac. The local reporters chatter among themselves, amazed at the international interest. The visitors exude edginess, ambition, insecurity and are eager as sprinters, desperate to jump the gun. They sit poised behind laptops, recorders and notebooks, texting and telephoning, scribbling down questions, scouring the internet for the latest updates. There is a clearing of the throat from de Massol, dazzled by camera flashes, and the proceedings begin. He defers to his superior from Paris, who defers to him to broadcast a scrap of video footage. It shows a man filling up at a Cognac petrol station. He is wearing a baseball cap and dark glasses and he pays in cash. As he drives off from the forecourt in the direction of the Grande Champagne, the number plate flashes into view, except the last figures are covered in mud. Assuming the correct assumptions have been made about the disguised numbers, this is a hire car, hired in Paris by a man who used false credentials. Needless to say the car has not been returned. De Massol, at his most self-important, informs the room that this man is professional, very dangerous and on the run. He must be over a border by now in Spain, Germany, Switzerland. The motives meanwhile are unclear. The police are ruling nothing out – neither a link with Middle Eastern politics nor a more random act of terror. The biggest puzzle is why this has happened in Cognac, which has lived through uninterrupted peace since the German occupation of the Second World War.

As de Massol speaks, he's dimly aware of a sound like the swarming of bees or some more sinister approaching menace as the journalists type furiously, even as their recorders turn and notes are scribbled. Then the questions begin. First ANN, eager for a sound-bite and not embarrassed to come out with a platitude that verges on an accusation. Indeed, the more provocative the better.

"So, sir, you're saying essentially you have very little to go on?"

De Massol hesitates, for all his careful preparation, not quite sure how much to disclose.

"We have a witness," he says. "The three-year-old daughter of the minister has survived. Of course, she is far too young to give any account, but over time, she may be able to give us some help.

The pack thrills with excitement. De Massol sees a sea of hands, demanding to know where she is. He cannot say. Is she hurt? Not physically.

And then they want motives, profiles, murder weapons. They want to know it all now and they need a coherent narrative for their insatiable editors seeking to satisfy their assumed version of an insatiable public. What they want to know instantly, is the work of hours of patient police work, which may or may not yield clear answers.

De Massol's Paris superior calls a halt after forty minutes of machine-gun fire questions, citing just that very need to get on with the patient police work. The journalists surge to the front of the room, wielding their recorders, microphones and notepads, greedy for yet more answers. De Massol is ushered out by his protective superior, nervous he will lose his nerve and start telling more than he ought. Mentioning the daughter wasn't exactly planned, but they would have found out. The problem is keeping her hidden away, but for now the pack is busy. Questions over, the processing has begun in a kind of reversal of the last forty minutes or so. Recorders are replayed, notebooks emptied, editors called, stories filed.

Living up to the cliché of their profession, at least some of them end up in the bar. The bar of choice is in a hotel called La Renaissance, where many of the hacks are staying. It's a faded three-star in one of the pedestrianised streets of the old town. La Renaissance refers to the first heyday of Cognac, during the era of Francois I. Gifted and intellectually curious, he was one of France's most promising kings until he clashed with his great rival the Holy Roman Emperor, and he was born in Cognac in a *château* that is now home to a rival brand to Cauvet, the reigning king of cognacs. La Renaissance hotel and bar resemble an old-style *château* only in their roomy discomfort. The bedrooms are large. The bathrooms are large as the owner has resisted all pressure to renovate. The downstairs bar is also grand in scale. A geographical anachronism, its high ceiling gives it the feel of a city, even a major port – Paris, Toulouse, Boulogne or Bordeaux – and represents the extent of Cognac's aspirations as the small-town headquarters of a global brand and its denizens' conviction they are cosmopolitan and their town is of international significance.

Behind a row of gleaming brass beer taps and in front of a mirrored wall of bottles stands mine host Bernard Granger. He is serving Pierre Barbier from the French news agency Agence France-Presse and Christian Lelans from Le Monde. They've set aside their rivalry, muted in any case as Le Monde is a client of the news agency, which churns out raw information for Le Monde to sift through and beautify, and they are sharing a beer. Pierre is dark and slim with the sallow complexion of someone who smokes and lives on coffee and adrenaline. He is wearing the jeans, T-shirt and a black leather jacket combination he first adopted as a teenager and that the codes of agency journalism have never forced him to slough off. The more leisurely Christian is smart-casual. Sometimes, he even wears a tie. In denial of the broken business-model of journalism, he still regards himself as a pillar of the French intellectual establishment. The deference of Bernard the host does not extend so far, but he is nonetheless delighted to entertain real-live Parisian journalists.

"It will never be solved, you know," he declares with unshakeable confidence as he hands them their beers.

"How do you know?" asks Pierre. "You're saying the police aren't up to it?"

"Possibly not, but even if they were. It's the perfect crime.

No-one was around. The only witness is three years old. Whoever did it must be in another country by now. There was a similar case years ago in the Alps. They even made a film about it. They found a family in an abandoned car, all shot dead and it remains a mystery. Most murders aren't solved, you know. It's just detective fiction to believe they are, like reading romantic novels and believing everyone can marry their one true love."

"Or believing everything you read in the press," says Christian, pre-empting his opinionated host. "And yet people love it regardless of whether it's true, just as they love village gossip."

"We can't just make it up though," says Pierre, honour piqued as the downtrodden agency reporter, who devotes so many all-but anonymous hours to trying to establish the basic facts, only for big-ego newspaper types to rewrite them and add their bylines. "There are libel laws."

"But journalism is an imperfect medium. Even if we don't libel, we cannot tell the whole truth. You could say that true art, however much a fiction, has a more essential truth than any transitory journalistic scoop," insists Christian, convinced he really should have been in academia but he has instead condescended generously to help a slightly wider public get to grips with a version of what's going on in the world. "We can't tell it exactly as it is. It would be unreadable as far as most people are concerned. They probably wouldn't even believe it. Most people don't want to know the truth unless it's palatable. They want to believe that when they die they go to heaven, their football team will win the world cup and that smoking and drinking are good for you because they enjoy them."

"Well, when it comes down to it, language is an imperfect medium and all communication is approximate," says the next customer who has sidled up to the bar. His accent is almost flawless. It's just about apparent to a French ear that he is not French, but it is almost impossible to tell where he is from.

"We get by," says Bernard, pulling his customer *une pression*, reluctant to be moving on from pet theories to abstractions that leave him cold.

His customer is Thomas, who happens to be Bénédicte's sister Dominique's *beau*. The attraction is a total mystery to Bénédicte, who tends to fall for suave, *bon chic bon genre* types. For reasons Bénédicte suspects are deep and bitter, the tall and pony-tailed Thomas has wilfully shrugged off his parents' *bourgeois* values, as Dominique is attempting to do. Already she has pledged to stand by his side in the green community they will set up in the Gironde once they have mustered the funds that so inconveniently are required. His theory is that the *Cognacais* and, by extension the *Bordelais* and *Girondais,* are perfectly suited to economic autarky. The architecture of the region, shuttered and surrounded by stone walls to protect their precious stocks of wine and *eaux-de-vie*, speaks of a deep-rooted desire to be self-sufficient, he posits, ignoring the equally deep-rooted desire to sell to the outside world at a discreet but significant profit. He would maintain that in any case arguments can only be pursued so far. Following them to their logical end leads to absurdity or madness. He seeks to base his behaviour on pushing arguments as far as he considers useful.

Meanwhile, he is continuing his research into the local community in the bar, made all the more interesting by the arrival of journalists, fresh from a press conference. One of his pastimes is trying to deduce just how much or how little of what the press reports is true and how successful the various powers are in keeping all meaningful information to themselves.

Thomas leaves Pierre and Christian to shoot the breeze with Bernard, now occupied in drawing diagrams of where the bodies were found. He prefers to introduce himself to the one woman journalist, sitting at a corner table with the man from ANN. It's the Anglo-Saxon section of the press corps. The ANN man is American. Polly is English, although based in Paris, working for Reuters, AFP's much bigger English-language rival, referred to by AFP as Rotters. She greets Thomas Fischer's arrival with what he interprets as English wariness, although she is not ungrateful for help in dealing with the ANN anchor, who has presented his card with a well-worn quip that a W is missing from his job title. Thomas swiftly manoeuvres Polly into French, even though his English is perfect. The ANN (w)anchor man decides it is expedient to head to his room for some editing and Thomas has Polly all to himself to debrief him on the press conference and little by little reveal almost all there is to know about her.

6

Francois, the namesake of Cognac's Renaissance king and ruler of Bénédicte's heart, during the week lives with his cousin Jeanne-Hélène and her mother, his Tante Simone in a Grande Champagne property, a stone's throw from the rather grander home of Bénédicte's family. When he is not working, Francois returns to his beloved Paris and indeed he had been there for the August 15th holiday, stretched into a long weekend. Escape to Paris is essential for Francois' well-being and yet he feels himself bound to Tante Simone and Cognac by what his family refers to as *une série noire*.

Tante Simone was married to Francois' father's brother Olivier. They met as students in Paris and might have stayed there and lived happily ever after. But soon after graduation, Simone's elder brother died in a plane crash and the grieving parents, desperate to hold on to their remaining child, suggested that Simone and Olivier should take on the property, promising all their help and contacts to smooth the way of the incoming Parisian. He would just be the manager. The real work would be done by those who knew how. For want of a better use for his philosophy degree, Olivier agreed. The young couple married in the village church on an idyllic summer's day and then set to ordering everyone else to work, while they got on with the job of providing the next generation. It did not take them long. Simone was swiftly pregnant and it seemed the void left by Simone's elder brother was about to be made less terrible. If only. The *série noire* continued with a still birth. Unable to believe their bad luck, Simone and Olivier sought to defy it. A year later, Simone was pregnant again. This time the baby, Jeanne-Hélène, survived, but the curse continued. A rare mixing of blood groups at birth caused brain damage. To the intellectual Olivier, it was the worst of fates. Unable to be philosophical, he blamed the doctors, the midwife, but above all himself. It suddenly seemed that his blood was never meant to be mixed with that of the Cognacais. In an act of selfish despair, or so it seemed to all the survivors, he hanged himself, leaving his widow to bring up a challenged child alone.

Francois had grown up with this story and his parents' insistence that everything possible should be done to support Tante Simone. His summer holidays were spent in the Cognacais countryside with his aunt and his cousin. Of all his family, Francois has proved the best able to cope with both and when a job came up at Cauvet, he did not hesitate to take it, not least because of a promise he could move to an Asian subsidiary after a year or two. His aunt impresses him for her lack of bitterness. He finds her stoical, fatalistic, understandably ready to believe the worst probably will happen, but also wise, warm and full of love for him. His cousin is undeniably unusual, and yet intriguing. Her days are spent working through obsessions. When other people would give up and get bored, she is content to labour over the same point for days, even weeks on end. Sometimes it is a question of studying and observing until she penetrates to a truth that supposedly more intelligent people fail to see. Sometimes, it is a question of persistent physical activity. There was a time when she adorned all the furniture with plaits made of wool and refused to abandon her self-assigned task until every chair leg and every door knob had a plait attached. If anyone removed one, she was quickly at work replacing it, like a spider with a broken web. In the vineyards where repetitive tasks are required, she is more useful than most people. Francois, though fast, Parisian and generally impatient, has always found it calming to introduce Jeanne-Hélène to a task and then leave her to carry it through over and over again, like winding a watch and leaving it to tick at its own steady pace.

After his return from his long Paris weekend, Francois

is subliminally aware that Jeanne-Hélène has acquired a new ritual, though he does not fully articulate it, at least not at first.

7

Stoical as she is, even Tante Simone needs a change of scene and, once in a while, Francois forgoes his Paris weekend to stay behind with Jeanne-Hélène and let his aunt take the high-speed train to the capital. Jeanne-Hélène is never happier than when she has her adored Francois to herself. Flattering as that is, Francois decides more varied society would do them both good and so he throws a party for everyone still around in the dog days of August and especially for Sophie and he is sufficiently lacking in tact - or is his most tragic flaw the family too-selfish-to-see-the-emotional-devastation-they-are-wreaking gene? - to ask Bénédicte if she could give her a lift as none of the summer guides has a car. Bénédicte, in the forlorn hope of stirring jealousy, asks if she can invite Paul as well as her sister and Thomas. Thomas in turn takes the view that a country party always needs guests and invites along his new friends from the journalists' corps – Polly, Pierre and Christian.

The party formula is simple but Francois hopes stylish – tender beef cooked (rare) over a fire of vine roots, followed by cheese and salad and he sets Jeanne-Hélène to work dipping strawberries in melted, high-quality dark chocolate, laced with cognac, by way of dessert. He imagines they'll eat, drink, dance and enjoy a summer evening in his aunt's garden.

In a hollow below the vineyards, the garden is overgrown and crowded with mature trees – figs, mulberries, walnuts. The story goes that his tragic uncle hanged himself from one of them. The trees all cast heavy shadows and need pruning or replacing, but Tante Simone either fails to notice, fails to care or has deeper reasons for leaving the trees as they are.

On the evening of the party, the heaviness of the air accentuates their melancholy. A storm could break at any moment.

The guests arrive in clusters: Bénédicte, Sophie, Paul, then Pierre, Christian, Polly, Thomas and Dominique, colleagues from Cauvet and neighbours from the Grande Champagne. Initially, the atmosphere is what the French call *crispé* and the English would characterise as full of embarrassing silences that leave Francois wondering guiltily why he didn't just stay quietly with Jeanne-Hélène, cook dinner with her and enjoy the companionable peace he knows she craves. But little by little, *apéritifs* are downed, the conversation begins to flow and the human need to share and process experience coalesces around the major news of the hour. The three journalists present wouldn't be able to believe their luck, if only the other two journalists weren't sharing it, as it emerges Paul and Bénédicte were first on the scene.

"How did you feel?" asks Polly, meaning to imply she is being ironically predictable, but she realises she has only confirmed everyone's worst fears of her profession.

"Shocked," says Paul, looking at her with derision and then he adds with the callousness of someone who knows all about capitalising on misfortune: "How would you feel? Or maybe that's a stupid question to a journalist who would see only the scoop."

Jeanne-Hélène is circling, handing round olives, peanuts, saying almost nothing, used to receiving little more attention than the furniture.

Thomas takes an olive and thinks how little he likes Paul. His aggressive retort to Polly is surely defensive. He starts asking broader questions, even though he knows most of the answers. What exactly is it that Paul does, what's he doing in Cognac, how long does he plan to stay? Surely the Saudi oil minister must have been slightly familiar to him. Maybe he even actually knew him, he suggests slyly.

Paul stares back, shaking his head almost imperceptibly, but takes the decision not to meet the challenge on this occasion. He puts a protective, possessive arm around Bénédicte and says they have gone through enough trauma. As he does so, he feels Bénédicte tense beneath his touch, not least because she is watching Francois move in on Sophie. She can't hear what he is saying, but she knows the routine. He'll be telling her he needs to improve his English and perhaps if he buys her dinner, she could give him a lesson or two. To the unbiased observer, the perfectly obvious situation can only head in one direction. Francois is not quite so confident, even though when they sit down at the table, Sophie has manoeuvred to sit beside him. Jeanne-Hélène has grabbed the chair on his other side, while Thomas is cosy next to Dominique, who is allowing him to expound his theories on a decadent, class-ridden society, and Bénédicte is between Pierre and Paul without really wanting to be, though she finds she likes Pierre, who seems to her too decent to be a journalist. He tells her he will probably return to Paris soon. There is no real justification to stay in Cognac unless there is a sudden major development or perhaps he can find the three-year-old daughter, not that she can tell him anything and he is no fan of that kind of snooping. Paul she distrusts. She wonders if that doubt has crept upon her since de Massol seemed to put him in the frame and meanwhile she senses the tension as he identifies Francois as a rival, another financial whizz at least as skilled as he is, but more scrupulous and more intellectual.

"If I held a party, it would begin in the afternoon," pronounces Paul. "Evenings take care of themselves, but the afternoon is the time when if I'm not actually working, I'm so bored I'm dangerous."

"That sounds like a threat," says Francois, replying in French to Paul's English. It's almost as if he is thinking out loud, rather than addressing Paul.

"Maybe it was," says Paul, replying in French, but then unable to continue and aware he has probably only succeeded in sounding odd to anyone who was listening. Most of the guests are busy passing around plates and meat in various stages of raw, slightly cooked and just about cooked. Any vegetarians, such as Polly, have to content themselves with salad and cheese.

"I heard that some people made money out of the murder of a very powerful oil minister and others lost millions," says Thomas, throwing down another gauntlet.

"Oh?" says Paul.

"Well, you would know. Isn't that what you do? Capitalise?"

"I trade and I'm on holiday."

"But still you know people who were trading?"

"Of course."

"You could have given them a call."

As the host, Francois feels the need to contain the rising tension, especially as the subject is an area of his expertise.

"The markets are still very volatile. Al-Asad was a safe pair of hands. They need to name his successor fast," he says. "But then volatility is a good challenge if you're a good trader. It was bad luck for the French they were all on holiday when the news broke, but I guess the City and the Americans did well."

Out of her depth and anxious to draw Francois' focus back to herself, Sophie declares she is starving and, picking up her knife and fork, wishes *"bon appétit"* to the assembled company, as if, thinks Bénédicte bitterly, she were mistress of the house. Any presumption entirely escapes Francois, who in keeping with Christian's not especially original argument that most people don't want inconvenient truths, is content at least for the purposes of this evening to have an idealised version of Sophie. The ambition, conceit and selfishness, fully apparent to Bénédicte and instinctively felt by Jeanne-Hélène, are lost on him. He sees only a beautiful English girl staring into his dark brown eyes. The cultural barrier adds to her charms as she asks him in wide-eyed wonderment how he manages to prevent Cauvet from losing millions to a sudden currency swing on a volatile market day. "It's extremely difficult," he smiles with a wink. "You have to be a mathematical genius."

Dominique sees it all too from what she regards as the safe-haven of her relationship with Thomas and in a rare, sisterly gesture, she sneaks around the table to Bénédicte and whispers to her: "Just make the most of the English guy. He's not bad looking, which is probably why Thomas doesn't like him."

Thomas' dislike is a positive spur to Bénédicte. She

considers Paul might be her only option for emerging from the evening with her pride intact. When the table is cleared and the furniture moved aside, she finds herself trying to teach an Englishman *ceroc*, while forcing herself not to notice Francois' far more graceful leading of Sophie, radiant with her sense of shared glamour, on to the makeshift dance floor.

Impatient with anything he cannot immediately master, Paul soon protests that it is too hot to be inside dancing and lures Bénédicte into the garden, where the wind is rustling through the too-mature trees. Bénédicte talks nervously, striving to fend off the potential for romance in the looming storm that in only slightly different circumstances she would relish. She points out the lights of her parents' house standing proud on the horizon and the direction of the spot where they found the bodies and in between the two, she tells him, is one of her very favourite places. "You'll laugh, I suppose, but the legend is that it is the true birthplace of cognac." "You'd better take me there, then," he says. "Can we walk?" They can. Recklessly, they do, as the gathering wind whispers through the vines and Paul tells Bénédicte the one good thing to come out of this tragedy is meeting her. Bénédicte says nothing. She's worrying the storm could be bad for her father's crop of *eau-de-vie* and she's worrying that she's only with Paul because Francois is with Sophie and that here she is walking with someone she doubts in virtual darkness to show him a ruined chapel upon which she has built dreams since her childhood. The sense of intimacy and fear and unreality is powerful, just as it was when together they stumbled across bullet-ridden bodies still warm but no longer breathing.

The chapel is nineteenth-century gothic, covered in ivy and battered by branches as the trees around begin to writhe, the moon disappears behind a cloud and the only light comes from the first flashes of lightning to race across the sky. The chapel's age alone is enough to contradict Bénédicte's story, but Bénédicte believes its emotional truth. The chapel, she declares in the manner of a tour guide, complete with very French English, is all that remains of the monastery where the noble Chevalier de la Croix Marron stayed one night and had a dream. He dreamt that the devil wanted to extract his soul and so he boiled him, but once was not enough. To extract the soul, he had to be boiled a second time. When he awoke, he told the monks of his dream. The monks were already distillers and to them it was immediately obvious what they had been doing wrongly. Instead of singly distilling the raw, young wine, if they wanted to extract its soul to make the *eau-de-vie* that eventually becomes cognac after long ageing in oak barrels, they would have to boil it, or distil it, twice. Double distillation was born. "You are laughing at me," Bénédicte observes at the end, realising that he has broken the spell and all the long-cherished romance of her secret chapel that couldn't stand up to a non-believing listener. He denies it. "It's a great story," he says. "But I think you'd have to boil me more than twice to extract any soul." "Whereas I wear mine on my sleeve," says Bénédicte. Paul isn't sure that is true, but he doesn't care. He dismisses psychological analysis and has cultivated a persona that avoids introspection. He has been known to brag about his reluctance to read fiction. He once glanced through a newspaper article that argued those who read lots of novels had more emotional empathy. Emotional empathy, he tells himself, would cramp his style. He is about to dare to kiss Bénédicte, but she is busy leading him into the deep gloom of the chapel. The *chevalier* is long gone. Instead, they realise with a start, they have found Jeanne-Hélène, on her knees praying in what you might describe as an ecstasy of despair before what is left of the altar. She is unaware of them until Paul speaks, urging them all away from a crumbling chapel, surrounded by trees as the lightning flashes ever more insistently. Jeanne-Hélène just resumes her frenzied praying, but he hoists her up and they make their way back, a strange uneasy trio, soon soaked to the skin, or the bones as the French would have it.

Polly has already called a taxi by the time the storm breaks and she's back in her unlovely hotel room, with its threadbare carpet and large, uncomfortable furniture.

Just as the strawberries dipped in chocolate and a bottle of cognac arrived, her editors called her with the unwelcome news that the ANN man has found the young witness. "So what. There is nothing a traumatised three-year-old can possibly say," thinks Polly, but she knows she has to placate them and now she's working on an explainer/throw-forward/follow/deep dive or some other crazy journalistic genre based on scraps of conversation at the party, in the bar, in the taxi and a general emptying of her notebook, which somehow she has to pass off as serious information. The hope to which she clings is that her forced flight might have made her more interesting to that charming host who seemed to have eyes only for the dreadful blonde English guide. Her fear is that yet another of the Saturday nights of her vanishing youth has served only to add to a global tide of fiction that passes itself off as fact.

Francois indeed has thought almost nothing of Polly, but his ardour for Sophie has also been dampened. With the return of the bedraggled Jeanne-Hélène, the latency of the early evening has given way to a general sense of being thwarted and that the party, which began with such potential, is an abortive failure. Jeanne-Hélène is no longer praying, but stammering and even Francois, so used to her ways, is unable to understand a word she says. That means she is stressed and he needs everyone to go home. The remaining guests are divided up among those with cars and Bénédicte finds herself once again taxi-ing Sophie and Paul, uncertain whether to be relieved that Sophie is not staying the night or furious to be so used, especially as she cannot avoid witnessing a tender goodbye as Francois slips his hand around Sophie's waist, pulling her close to deliver *bises,* which promise so much more, and whispers *"à très bientôt".*

Bénédicte then leads her charges to her battered old Peugeot and tells them she will take Paul to his house first and drop off Sophie last on the basis she is staying closest to her own central Cognac flat. Logistically, it makes sense. Romantically, the plan is designed to postpone Paul's advances. Paul sits lusting and plotting in the front next to her, Sophie sits smitten and sulking in the back and they drive along in silence as the rain pelts down.

They are part-way down the single-track road that leads to Paul's house when Paul yells stop and Bénédicte slams on the brakes. The car swerves violently and she just avoids hitting a deer. Clumsy and bewildered, it looks at them in reproach with its huge sylvan eyes and tears into the night and Bénédicte bursts into uncontrollable tears. They are the tears bottled all evening and for days before. It's Paul's big opportunity to put his arm around her.

"You'll have to drive," she sobs. "I can't." He's drunk too much to want to go far, he says. After all, the only reason he had accepted a lift in the first place was so he could get plastered. The solution is they all stay with him this evening. He has plenty of room and they are almost there.

8

De Massol likes to work on Sunday mornings. He takes his mind off the emptiness of his weekends and gives himself the sense he is thoroughly on top of the week ahead as he collects his thoughts in an office deserted but for a bare minimum of duty staff. The only evidence of most of his colleagues is in the form of the unwashed coffee cups, family photos, pictures drawn by their children, jars of pens and piles of notebooks strewn about their desks and viewed by him with distaste. His own desk is clinically neat – computer, telephone, pen and notepad. He also has a whiteboard, inspired by the many detective dramas he has watched, which in turn must have had some flimsy basis in established procedure, and he stands before it and maps out the little he knows. He sketches the murder scene, near the properties of the Rivet family and Tante Simone, and then he lists the characters so far. There is the oil minister, apparently just passing through as an honoured guest of the Cauvet family, there is the Cauvet family, supposedly above suspicion – what could they possibly have to gain from the disastrous publicity of a murder in the Grande Champagne? And there is Castaniet. De Massol has yet to fathom Gilles Castaniet, the latest of the long line of Castaniets to hold the ultimate Cauvet job, or his wife, the immaculate Marie Castaniet, who heads the company's public relations department, responsible for organising al-Asad's visit as well as overseeing the summer guides. As much as the Cauvets, the Castaniets have no interest in negative PR. Still de Massol distrusts them. Even by his exceptional standards of orderliness, they are unnaturally well presented and controlled, Gilles Castaniet in his pure, white tasting cabinet, totally undisturbed every morning, and his wife in Dior and Chanel, never a hair out of place, holding sway over the summer guides with the iron discipline and absence of affection of a stepmother. In the only dealings with each other de Massol has seen, he has observed scrupulous, if not strained politeness as if they are strangers. The most natural thing about them is Gilles' dog Napoléon, a black Labrador, though even he seems to have been trained into perfect obedience. They have no children. That is hardly a crime, but noteworthy considering that the Castaniets have been providing tasters for the Cauvet house for generations. Gilles Castaniet, barring any scandalous revelations, is the last.

Whereas the Castaniets behave as if they are strangers, Bénédicte and Paul most decidedly seem far too familiar, though de Massol has yet to learn that they are under the same roof. He has no evidence they had ever been together before they met at the scene of the crime, but he senses complicity. He has also discovered Paul's trading network made a mint in the days following al-Asad's murder, already reason enough to arrest him as far as he is concerned, but the *laissez-faire* London regulators say they can find nothing unusual: many traders made money on the minister's demise, others lost it in a week of choppy trading. In the total absence of any incriminating evidence, it is better to leave him at large unsuspecting and with all borders on alert just in case.

Then there is the three-year-old survivor. If only she could tell him what she knew. After ANN's regrettable discovery of her, de Massol has had her transferred to Paris under expert care. He reasons she will be less visible in the capital than in small-town Cognac and is happy enough to let Paris continue the efforts to work out whether there is anything at all she can tell them.

The other leads are just as tenuous. He has noticed Thomas Fischer stalking the journalists with more than ordinary curiosity and fleetingly entertains the idea that an anti-society, anti-capitalist environmentalist might have taken out the world's most powerful oil minister in a vineyard and as a bonus found relish in the damage inflicted to the image of an aristocratic, luxury French product. But then it's equally likely that the CIA decided they had finally had enough of producers' cartels and engaged a hit man.

Disgusted with his lack of progress, he grabs his car keys and heads off to the see the family of the murdered chauffeur, regardless of the fact it is Sunday and of the rawness of their grief.

Polly is ahead of him. She hates herself. She is just following orders. One of her editors knew someone who knew someone and as a result, he has provided her with the address, implying that she is an utter fool for failing to get hold of it herself.

She knows as soon as she arrives that she has found the right house. It's one of a community of homes built for modest families. Unable to afford the beautiful stone properties in the countryside or in the old town centre, they bought patches of land near the cemetery on the edge of Cognac and had piles of breeze blocks dressed up in pebble-dash built upon them. The tombs in the cemetery have greater style.

The house's shutters, the modern, roll-down kind, are tightly shut. The silence is unnatural, but the car parked in the driveway, lacking its chauffeur, implies occupancy, as do children's plastic toys abandoned on a patch of grass. Polly jangles the bell – an incongruous, nerve-grating metal bell with a chain, which must have come from some previous family home or perhaps a souvenir from a holiday somewhere. Slowly the door opens and a woman, who can only be the lyrically-named Sylvie Rossignol, tells her: "You had better come in." She does not ask who she is. She instinctively seems to know. Is it because the ANN man has yet again managed to get there first? Polly begins apologising, offering her deepest condolences, feeling all the time like a vulture, feeding off grief. She follows Mme Rossignol into the darkened main room and the widow raises one of the shutters, letting in shafts of light in which the dust particles swirl. "He meant everything to me," Mme Rossignol says, as if singing from her tragic nightingale heart, thinks Polly, remembering Oscar Wilde's devastating short story. Polly has arrived at the precise moment when grief needs an outlet. "And the worst of it is I never told him I loved him." "I'm sure he knew," says Polly, thinking she has no right to be hearing this. It's meant for a priest not a hack. "And then there are the children, so young they won't even remember him." Polly can say nothing to that. She has heard they are five and three – three just like al-Asad's little girl even though al-Asad was so very much older than his murdered chauffeur. "The strange thing is, he really hadn't wanted to drive that man," the widow muses. "The other drivers had been really jealous of Michel for being chosen, but he was worried about it. He didn't seem to mind picking him up at the airport, but after that he was reluctant. He said something was going to go wrong. It was very unlike him. He wasn't naturally gloomy. He was used to being discreet, hearing things and saying nothing. But this time he seemed burdened." Polly's ears prick up. She has her angle. "Did he say what he thought would go wrong?" He didn't. Of course not, thinks Polly. His wife had just told him not to be so superstitious and that the job was a great honour.

Polly has enough for some sort of half-baked story and she is only too glad to take her leave. As she walks down the driveway, de Massol walks up it.

While he chips away, unfeeling in his pursuit of whatever had been bothering Michel, Sophie and Bénédicte are confronting each other as the coffee machine splutters in Paul's kitchen. Paul has yet to surface and his guests have decided to fend for themselves or rather Sophie has assumed the right to get coffee under way and Bénédicte has acquiesced, though resolutely persevering in English, while Sophie endeavours to vaunt her French. *"Francois est très sympa,"* she declares. *"Tu sais s'il a déjà une copine? De beaux mecs comme ca ne sont jamais célibataires,"* she crashes on, with all the worldly wisdom of a twenty-two year old. For Bénédicte, it's the emotional equivalent of fingernails on a blackboard. "I don't think there is anyone serious," Bénédicte says in English, wishing she had the cunning to lie, as if it would make any difference. "I think that coffee is ready," is all she can think of saying to prevent Sophie confiding more of her crush. "I'll take some to Paul." And so appearing far more devoted than she actually is, she arrives in Paul's bedroom with morning coffee and places it on a rickety wooden table that he had acquired with the house, along with all its other furniture. *"Je t'aime,"* he says. "I suppose that's your legendary British humour," says Bénédicte. "Sometimes we jest in earnest," he says. Bénédicte doesn't understand but then he didn't really mean her to.

Francois' conversations with Jeanne-Hélène are almost a collision of languages. They rely on a narrow strip of shared vocabulary that unites their radically different thought patterns. Today, they are both clearing up *chez* Tante Simone and today Jeanne-Hélène is calm. The storm has passed and with it the frantic praying and the stuttering. They are back to their old relationship in which Jeanne-Hélène adores her talented, handsome cousin, relishing that for today at least he is hers. As they stack away plates, glasses, cutlery, Jeanne-Hélène musters all her courage. "Don't like Sophie," she says. "Don't like Sophie," she repeats. Francois carries on stacking. "But she likes you," he says, placatory. "Don't like Sophie," Jeanne-Hélène insists. Francois knows his only weapon if winning Sophie really matters to him is to distract Jeanne-Hélène or the obsession with dislike will grow and grow, touching every corner of the household, just like the plaits. "Sophie's just an ordinary girl. She wants ordinary things. You're special. You see the world as no-one else does. You have rare things to give. You don't have to get caught up in its desperate pursuit of just having the same things as everyone else – husband, children, career. You have the freedom to just be yourself, seeing the world in your unique way." This is a major speech and Jeanne-Hélène is indeed briefly distracted, but not won. "But you want ordinary things?" she asks after a long pause. "That's not certain," says Francois. "I like the idea of giving up the world." "Giving up the world with Sophie?" asks Jeanne-Hélène. Childlike, she aims straight as an arrow for the truth. "I think Sophie wants the world," he says. And, of course, he wants to give her the world, to be her world, but he isn't exactly teasing Jeanne-Hélène. He is not simply insincere. He has his spiritual side. He has read Gide and adored *La Porte Etroite*. Melancholy Cognac and Tante Simone and Jeanne-Hélène – just as much as glittering Paris and ambition, as yet boundless – are the basis of his mental furniture.

However incomplete, the understanding between Jeanne-Hélène and Francois is rooted in an emotional warmth entirely absent from the Sunday charade *chez les* Castaniets. Sunday is when, after mass, they sit down to formal lunch, occasionally with carefully-selected guests. Today *M. et Mme le Maire* are being served champagne and canapés to whet their appetite for leg of mutton pricked with rosemary and garlic to be accompanied with an excellent Bordeaux selected by the *maître-de-chai*. *M. et Mme le Maire*, compared with the Castaniets, verge on the vulgar. They both like to gossip and all the savour of the Castaniets' invitations derived from what they might reveal about a murdered minister.

"What were the al-Asads like?" they want to know.

"Well," ponders Gilles, taking a delicate sip of champagne, "al-Asad was a brilliant man and his young, self-effacing wife accompanied him, giving absolutely nothing away of herself. There's not much to say."

"Oh come, Gilles," coaxes *Monsieur le Maire*. "You can do better than that."

"I'm not sure I can unless you want me to tell you that I felt in a strange way we overlapped. He sold his barrels of oil to refineries, which essentially do little more than boil it and then sell it to people like us, while I blend *eaux-de-vie* after it has been distilled and aged in barrels," Gilles says, and adds after a pause. "Now he has left the world oil market sorely in need of a successor."

Madame Castaniet, unhappy with the way the conversation is turning, leads them to her exquisitely laden table.

"Ah, *chère* Marie, how do you manage it?" gushes *Madame le Maire*.

"*Ah Juliette, il s'agit juste d'un déjeuner très simple.*"

And with that, she gives Gilles the order to carve.

AUTUMN

9

Lumbering *vendangeurs*, ungainly machines that have replaced deft human hands, lollop along Cognac's winding tracks after days spent shaking the vines and sending the grapes raining down, ripe to become rough wine pending distillation in the gleaming stills that will soon belch out steam like mist into the crisp autumn air.

The summer tourists and, with them the summer guides, have dispersed. Sophie has left with a confident stride and a toss of her blond hair for an internship in Paris, where, as Bénédicte is so painfully aware, Francois spends most of his weekends.

Paul has also fled for now, with a promise to be back soon and stay in touch, but Bénédicte senses he has thrown himself into his old habits of fast trading and fast drinking, seeking oblivion from recent shocks. He has sent her an email or two, one with a link to a newspaper article that names him as the first person on the scene, together with a

French heiress, as she has been cast. It also speculates that, as a trader, Paul Gray would have been familiar with the Saudi oil minister and could have profited from the market gyrations that followed his death. Paul himself is quoted as saying that he makes it a rule never to speak to the press. Even to Bénédicte, reading through the filter of a foreign language, that line comes across as pompous or guilty or both. Bénédicte recalls the force with which he laid into the English journalist at Francois' party and wonders what exactly was behind it. If she knew him any better, if she could put him in context, she could theorise that someone of his background, handed out advantages and effortlessly made a part of the financial status quo would instinctively distrust the disruptive glare of the press. Alternatively, she might simply put his edgy, defensive aggression down to a guilty conscience.

Bénédicte, as her sister would be the first to observe, is hardly anti-establishment herself, at least not in any articulate way. She strives to conform, and yet like many a woman working in a world in which men made the rules, she is an outsider, by turns dreamy, romantic, naïve, embarrassing, not least when she's right. Despite decades of feminism and female academic achievement, her life is based on the tacit assumptions men will be promoted above her and take the key decisions. An equal relationship with a man might be forever out of reach. The very design of the offices where she works seems to make that point.

As she muses over whether to reply to Paul, she is lingering unwisely in the *couloir de la direction*, which is a short cut, just about tolerated as long as not abused, from her office to the newer wing of the building, which houses Francois and the rest of the financial team, along with the advertising department and the company archives. The directors' corridor is where Cauvet's six directors, all men, have ownership of palatial offices they rarely occupy, while their ever-present secretaries, all women, are crammed into one room, which is modest but vibrant. There is always a vase of flowers, often a home-made cake they take it in turns to bring in and they've clubbed together for a kettle so they can make coffee to sustain them through the marathon crises that unfold when their bosses decide at a minute's notice to jet off to the other side of the world. At the end of the corridor is a boardroom with a giant table polished so highly that the directors are reflected in it as they sit around reflecting in their giant leather chairs. Bénédicte knows that from previous glimpses into a room that reminds her of the best parlour at home in its cold, formal, rarely-used, away- from- the- normal- and- everyday atmosphere, and she's not convinced it can foster the best decisions. Today the doors, with their gleaming brass handles, are closed. All six directors are in town and they are in conference. She hurries guiltily past and is half-way down the stairs at the other end of the corridor as Anne, one of the secretaries, begins to climb up. Much as Bénédicte prides herself on not being a gossip, she finds herself eager to know the subject of the day's conference. After the usual greetings, she dares to ask. Anne says she doesn't know why they are meeting, but she lets slip that de Massol had telephoned the previous day. There might be a connection.

De Massol has indeed learnt more from the grieving widow than Polly had fathomed in her journalistic haste. On the other hand, Polly has a manageable story. De Massol has only potentially libellous fragments whose meaning may elude him forever. He knows that Michel Rossignol overheard a conversation in which al-Asad seemed to be talking with Cauvet about a distribution agreement. Such deals, he has learnt, are common practice in the drinks world as one brand sees the commercial logic of helping to distribute another not-quite-competitor brand, but Rossignol had been stunned to hear a Muslim oil minister mention the possibility of providing sales opportunities for a forty per cent spirit. Equally, why on earth need Cauvet entertain such an idea when the massive Asian market beckoned? Madame Rossignol knew little more. Her husband had only mentioned a scrap of conversation in passing and she had thought little of it until de Massol's insistence that anything she could recall might help.

Now the directors are arguing over it. They are Castaniet and two representatives of the Cauvet family, father and son, standing for the traditional hierarchy, plus three other directors, two imposed by the group that owns

Cauvet and a brilliant, still young English salesman, Clive Furness, who has soared through the ranks to become the youngest ever board member. The distribution agreement was his idea. Castaniet had always hated it. The others had liked its sheer audacity and dismissed Castaniet as overly fastidious, more of an artist than a businessman. They pointed out he had always opposed the Asian market because he thought the drinking habits – down the hatch with a cry of *yam seng* – failed to do justice to Cauvet's centuries of revered tradition. Now Asia is the biggest revenue earner, Castaniet has to admit that. But Cauvet is not complacent. Who knows what the future holds? It's worth having footholds everywhere, even if the Middle East is off the agenda for now.

What de Massol needs to know is: if the driver and his wife knew about the plan, who else did and could it possibly be a motive for murder?

10

Ironically, given the Cauvets' scramble for secrecy, lots of people know and most of them have no intention of doing anything strategic with the information. Sophie heard it mentioned and she is busy passing it on to Francois as they lie, decadent on a stolen Friday afternoon, in his apartment in Le Marais. A stone's throw from la Place des Vosges, Francois' self-consciously stylish Paris pad has exposed brick walls and a sleek black floor in dichotomy with the brick's roughness. It's also a counter statement to Tante Simone and her heavy Cognac furniture and cosy clutter. Francois is vaguely processing the contrasts of his life as Sophie prattles happily on. Relaxing into their intimacy, she has lapsed into *ingénue* innocence, to some tastes, more charming than her cultivated cool. "I found it really odd," she's saying. "You know that oil minister, he was talking to the English director, that guy Furness, about selling cognac in Saudi Arabia and I thought they weren't allowed to drink, though the minister certainly did." "It couldn't have been a serious suggestion," Francois murmurs, only half listening. "If it were, I'd see the figures turn up." "It sounded serious to me," says Sophie, miffed at the insinuation she could get anything wrong.

Paul knew too. He is even recklessly airing such potentially useful knowledge in public in a Canary Wharf bar. It's barely four o'clock in the afternoon and he has lost count of how many beers he has consumed. Some part of him knows he should not relinquish control, but the desire to do so is the greater force, so he drinks on, not as an alcoholic, not with enjoyment but to lose himself. His co-drinker is a co-trader, who trades by the name of Bart. Both have almost forgotten he was ever christened anything else. They have a one hundred per cent record of trading on the right side of any output decision made by OPEC for as long as al-Asad was in charge and they are lamenting that their lucky mascot is no more. It has been a very good run. They don't need to trade any more. The problem is they haven't found anything better to do. It's a drug, it's a habit and they cannot think beyond it.

"There is one play I don't think anyone's thought of," Paul slurs.

"Oh yeah," says Bart.

"Al-Asad was on to something when he copped it." Paul takes another gulp or two and waits to be prompted.

"Go on..."

"Those cognac dealers were trying to sell in Saudi. Imagine the margins to be made on illegal booze in a desert."

"Even for me, that's high risk," says Bart, almost soberly.

"Maybe they've got bored with the obvious places."

"But how would you trade on it especially without the main man?"

"Requires thought," Paul mutters.

Thomas Fischer knew too but the fact is filed in the corner of his brain where he stores damaging information about the smug establishment. For now, he is enjoying the moment he is in with very little calculation. It's a glorious autumn day and he and Dominique are riding through the pine forests of Les Landes. They've ridden for hours, each locked in their own thoughts, breathing in the smells of pine and earth and autumn. Dominique is remembering horse rides gone by when they went out *en famille*, her parents behind, Dominique and Bénédicte galloping ahead. She and Bénédicte are equals on horseback, both natural horsewomen without fear or insecurity, effortlessly in control, in harmony with everything around them. The sibling rivalry ebbs away. Neither has to prove to the other that her approach to life is more valid, her intellect more powerful or her looks more enticing. But since Dominique met Thomas, the sisters have ceased to ride together and lost their best connection, a fact Dominique articulates to herself as Thomas rides beside her with merely the competence he brings to everything. Thomas has no siblings. He was a cherished late child to a protective mother with an iron will, which he respected and resisted in equal measure. His father by comparison was weak. Born into land-locked, middle European, middle-class comfort, he had none of Frau Fischer's fierce determination. Everything came to him easily before he realised he wanted it and his money somehow spawned more money. The partial exception was fatherhood, but even then, he had been content to be childless for as long as life was pleasant, while his wife had sunk deeper and deeper into the gloom of the most personal of failures in a conservative community that saw no validity for women beyond motherhood. After Thomas arrived, his mother had a few years of intense fulfilment until intense anxiety kicked back in. The trigger - though had it not been that, it would have been something else - was the murder of one of Thomas' supposedly best friends, the son of a near neighbour with whom Thomas had spent many slightly strange hours in his mother's concern to offset the isolation of her only child. To Thomas, in hindsight, the murder made perfect sense. Karl's family seemed at best indifferent to his well-being. Was it surprising it should somehow lose him?

He had only once been inside Karl's house. Most of their camaraderie had been based on cycle rides followed by hearty meals provided by Frau Fischer at the Fischers' cosy, well-managed home, where the only parental fault was to love too much. Karl never suggested returning the hospitality, but at Thomas' unfeeling persistence, he one day led Thomas to where he lived. Motionless autumnal trees, standing in mouldering leaves that Thomas' father would have raked into orderly piles, surrounded a tall narrow 1930s house. No-one was inside to welcome them. Instead, Karl had taken a key from round his neck to open the front door. The house felt unaired. The hallway was a narrow strip between rows of doors that gave on to small, dark rooms overly filled with dated furniture. Thomas came close to experiencing something like guilt for insisting on what felt like an invasion into the shamefully unenviable. Karl said his father was away on a business trip. He was a salesman. His mother was a nurse and worked evenings and nights. His elder brother and sister, who, to the fascination of the isolated Thomas, were twins, had left home. Karl said he hoped to do the same as soon as he could. It only occurred to Thomas later that he should have asked why. Perhaps the house itself with all its darkness and emptiness had seemed reason enough. In any case, Karl seemed to regret the confidence. After it, Thomas returned to his own loving family and by unspoken, mutual consent, rarely saw Karl again. Karl really did run away only to reappear in a newspaper article as a murder victim, the most shocking event of Thomas' life so far, not least because of the impact on his own freedom. Instead of sympathy for bereaved parents, Frau Fischer focused all her selfish love on protecting her son. If the murder had logic for Thomas, it made no sense at all to his mother. The only fate she could imagine to be worse than having a murdered son would be to have a son who turned into a murderer. From then on, she barely allowed Thomas out of her sight until he too one day left home, spitefully and completely. It hadn't really mattered where he went, but he needed not to be defined by what he saw as the unhealthy confines and exaggerated emotional bonds among which he had grown up. He took himself to university and then casual teaching jobs in various parts of the world and now somehow, through a chain of circumstances, he is in *la France profonde*, where he strains destructively for the very opposite of its deeply-rooted, *appellation controlée* attachment to *terroir*.

Dominique is beside him on her horse Caspar, suddenly aware of how little she knows about the man she thinks she wants to spend her life with. She's made it a badge of honour that Thomas seeks to have no history and to belong nowhere. He is a neutral force. But her emotional needs are more conventional than she would ever admit to Thomas or to Bénédicte.

"Don't you love it here?" she asks, almost as a provocation. He smiles with ill-concealed effort and says they should get back to Cognac. Deflated, discouraged, disheartened, she agrees.

As it's the weekend, Tante Simone has Jeanne-Hélène to herself. She too has noticed the new praying ritual. New is a slight exaggeration. Jeanne-Hélène has always had a tendency to knot herself into longing over things she wants to happen and things she does not want to happen and even things that have happened that she wants to undo, perhaps requiring the memories of countless acquaintances to be wiped clean as if an amnesia potion could be poured into their coffee or cognac. She has spent years expending vast amounts of energy wishing for impossible victories – that pet rabbits should live forever, that the dentist would declare her teeth perfect even though she grinds them every night, that Francois will always remember to come back from Paris. In a refusal to accept the things to which most people resign themselves, she has constructed entire imaginary worlds based on how she thinks things should be. Of late, however, her outbreaks of praying have taken on a terror and pathology. Tante Simone suspects Francois' love-sickness and his Paris weekends that increasingly stretch into the week are the cause. She endeavours to broach the subject as they gather walnuts in the muddle of the overgrown garden.

"Is there something wrong, my angel?" asks Tante Simone. Jeanne-Hélène peels away the outer casing around a gnarled, ancient-looking walnut shell, turning her hands filthy brown with walnut oil.

"Lots wrong," she says after a pause.

"Lots?" echoes Tante Simone. "Lots and lots? Then we'd better make some tea and talk about it in the kitchen."

She leads her daughter in from the cold autumn air and sets the basket of nuts on the kitchen table, which is associated in her mind with some of the huge discussions of her life. Around the enduring table, over coffee, over wine, over dinner, she has faced a future without a husband, made funeral arrangements with the local priest and come to terms with Jeanne-Hélène, the end of her particular line who denies her the mother's indulgence of a second chance to enjoy youth and beauty. What she gives instead is much rarer if only anyone can fathom her instinctive, prescient knowledge.

Tante Simone pours out verbena herbal tea and watches Jeanne-Hélène cradle her cup for its precious warmth.

"So what's wrong?" she coaxes.

"Lots. Everything."

"But something new? Can you tell me or is it a secret?"

"A secret."

Jeanne-Hélène will tease now. Previous experience suggests she will nurse her inner-most wound for hours, maybe days, almost enjoying the pain. Tante Simone is deciding to give up when Jeanne-Hélène takes her by surprise with a promise that she will show her the secret tomorrow.

Tomorrow is a misty Sunday. In heavy coats and boots, early in the morning, they trudge through damp fields and autumn leaves to the chapel where Bénédicte and Paul found Jeanne-Hélène weeks ago. Like Bénédicte, Tante Simone grew up with the story of the *chevalier* and his double distillation dream, but unlike Bénédicte she dismissed it as errant nonsense. Outside the chapel, a black Labrador is tethered to a tree. If he were left there to keep guard, the goal is missed as Jeanne-Hélène and he greet each other as friends and almost silently. "*Bonjour Napoléon*," she whispers, patting the velvet top of his head and then putting her other hand to Tante Simone's mouth to stop her exclaiming. "Shhh," she says, leading her mother through the undergrowth to peer into the chapel. Inside are the dog's master Gilles Castaniet and Thomas Fischer in tender embrace. Tante Simone gasps. Apparently, they are too engrossed to notice. She instinctively retreats, pulling Jeanne-Hélène with her. Her mind is racing. She suspects Castaniet and Fischer will realise they had been seen. She needs quickly to be away from pursuit and not walking on damp grass where every footprint lingers. They scamper through a tangle of brambles and ancient woodland and then zig-zag on to one of the limestone paths that separate the vineyards and run helter-skelter home.

Tante Simone is in shock and yet it's as if she half knew. The barren perfection of Castaniet's outward relations with his wife suddenly makes sense. But Fischer is a puzzle. He has to have a motive, she believes. "You mustn't let it upset you, my angel," she tells her daughter as soon as she has recovered her breath. Even as she says it, she holds the conviction that this isn't the real secret. She's sure it has disturbed Jeanne-Hélène for whom other people's relations are a cruel reminder of the many things she is denied in life, but a mother's instinct tells her there is more. This is just the secret Jeanne-Hélène felt able to share and it was far easier for her to show it than to tell it.

Although Sunday morning is usually the time when de Massol likes best to work, on this particular morning, the prospect of another day of thwarted investigation in Saudi Arabia after a night of very little sleep has no appeal. When he should have been sleeping, he was wretched with food poisoning in his strange hotel room furnished with human-sized Barbie doll furniture, white with ornate gold handles. Now he faces futile meetings with officials in Jeddah, the Red Sea port where the Saudi oil minister and his family had been staying just before leaving for France. That and the Saudi view that Jeddah is more welcoming to foreigners than Riyadh – that is, more liberal – are the joint reasons for de Massol to be drained and nauseous in this particular tract of desert heat outside and Arctic air-conditioning inside. De Massol has been promised that high-level ministry staff will come to him. In reality, he has been chauffeured between hotel lobbies and shopping malls, where ice-cream parlours are regarded as suitable meeting places. For the local population, they are clearly *the* place in which to flirt, in so far as such things are allowed. De Massol is dimly aware he is caught in the cross-hairs of intricate phone texting as young girls stroll back and forth, wearing *abayas* with hoods that reveal at least as much rich, raven-black hair as they conceal.

Top of the agenda today is al-Asad's former *aide*. This meeting is in a formal restaurant on the edge of the Red Sea. It's expensive, with starched white table cloths, lobster on the menu and very few customers. The nearby beach is just as deserted. De Massol, blinking in sunlight made more dazzling by a wall of windows designed to maximise the sea view, says he can only manage mineral water. The *aide*, who tells de Massol to just call him Muhammed, orders chicken and rice, plus an accompanying Coke, and tucks in with alacrity. *"Bon appétit,"* de Massol murmurs, wincing at the Coke and trying not to breathe in the smell of the chicken.

If Muhammed knows anything about his former boss's killer, it's clear his aim, just like that of everyone else de Massol has met in Jeddah, is to keep it to himself. His sense is the oil market is the only thing that cares al-Asad is dead and no-one, not even his wife is screaming for justice. Perhaps they think his death is justice.

"Tell me what al-Asad was like," ventures de Massol.

"He was a brilliant man. He is greatly missed," Muhammed says, between mouthfuls.

"And his successor? Is he also a brilliant man?"

"It will be a very smooth transition," Muhammed says.

"And al-Asad, did he have any enemies?" de Massol perseveres, delicately sipping his mineral water.

"Perhaps his number one wife," Muhammed says, unexpectedly winking in what seems to be a rather exaggerated attempt to show he is not serious.

"And apart from work, what else did he do? Did he have hobbies? What was he doing here?"

"Visiting the university. He'd invested some of his own money in it. It was his passion to have a legacy. He was even paying the university to research renewable technology. Not everyone agreed with that as you can imagine."

De Massol decides he has some kind of lead and summons the waiter for the bill. Muhammed insists he must pick up the tab. "You only had water," he protests. De Massol is too weak to argue. He wonders if he might even be hallucinating in his sleep-starved, sun-dazzled state as he spots a Cauvet bottle tucked beside the reception counter as he staggers out. It is in any case empty, but intriguing nonetheless.

11

Polly also works Sundays – and Saturdays and evenings and nights. She always has. At school, at university, now as a journalist driven not by worldly ambition so much as by a semi-articulated desire to continue burying herself in sentences. It's an ingrained habit she cannot break. Too late, she realises she needs also to have something head-line grabbing to say that her editors and supposedly the wider world wish to hear. Maybe she should have been a medieval monk content anonymously to write manuscripts in the silence of a high-vaulted library, humbly convinced only the Divine could perceive the whole truth, and that she should draw all worldly pleasure from sunlight shafting in to illuminate the gilded edges of the page. Instead, she sits before her computer, beneath a low ceiling, oppressed by the weight of other people's achievements and the expectations generations of feminism have brought to bear. To her, the sisterhood seems only to have added to the pressures. It has fuelled aspiration but failed to provide answers. At the age of thirty-three, she has no idea how to accomplish the published novelist-, prize-winning correspondent- and motherhood-status of which her contemporaries crow in the Christmas round robins she dreads. If she weren't so painfully aware that it is only fiction, she could console herself with the thought that the accomplishments of Jane Austen's heroines were modest – others were better pianists, less prone to misjudgements and more diligent letter-writers – and for all that, it was the Elizabeth Bennetts and Emma Woodhouses who got the men of their dreams and got on with their biological and social destiny. Polly doesn't even have a boyfriend/partner/lover/significant other. She blames her parents, the quiet, middle-class parents who gave her a perfectly happy childhood, while implicitly encouraging conformity and explicitly presenting excessive ambition and arrogant self-belief as dangerous, even evil. Defiantly, but not boldly enough, she has veered from the path they would have wished her to pursue as a teacher, or a small-town lawyer and above all, a mother, after marriage in a white lace dress at the local church to the boy next-door. Now here she is, no longer fit for what she was born for or the lot she has strived for, staring at a computer screen, clamped into an artificial need that precludes quality thought. It can only be her desperation for some kind of scoop, she tells herself, that impels her to pick up the phone and dial the number of Pierre, whose card she has kept at the top of a stack on her desk for weeks. He is of course a rival, but she suggests they should pool resources over a drink. To her surprise he agrees. He just has to finish a story and then he'll be at Le Temps Perdu. Does she know it? She does, she says, putting her trust in Google out of sudden shyness not deceit. She is sunk if Paris has more than one bar named Le Temps Perdu.

Lucky in the small, unimportant things, Polly is blessed in that there is only one and it's in a cobbled, lop-sided street near the elegant Palais Royal, where the lawyers of the Conseil d'Etat reside and the *beau monde* frequents the Comédie Francaise. Pierre, wearing his trademark leather jacket, arrives as Polly does. They almost bump into each other and in the moment of confusion, he somehow grabs her by her elbow and kisses her on each cheek. *"Comment ca va?"* he asks. *"Ca va,"* she replies, blushing deeply and they wander in.

Le Temps Perdu is cave-like, thinks Polly, juggling French and English in her head. It's like an English cave and a French cellar – dark, almost window-less, drawing you in, down to the low-ceilinged inner limits. They take a table at the back and order glasses of mediocre red wine, delivered with a dish of peanuts. Polly asks if Pierre has seen Christian and he wants to know whether she has seen "the guy from ANN". "I've run into him a few times and he's still as over-bearing," says Polly. Pierre smiles. Christian is not overbearing, just lazy and smug. "Do we just have all the moral high-ground and nothing to show for it?" asks Polly. "What do you mean?" he asks and Polly retreats. A sip of red wine and she has been too much herself. Too much the martyr and assuming too much about Pierre. All she knows is that they are both agency reporters. "I just feel I'm working away for nothing," she says. "My editors want stories I can't in honestly deliver. They want to know who murdered al-Asad now and they think I'm useless because I don't know more than the police do or let's face it, a fraction as much and even they are fairly unlikely to get to the truth and it's far more disastrous if they don't." "We only observe and I'm happy with that choice. We have half a chance of managing to do that," says Pierre. Polly wonders what he's thinking about this bitter English girl, exaggerating, overstating, making too much fuss. The chemistry is dispersing, despite her still-tingling elbow. She reproaches herself for yet another romantic defeat. "They say I should be setting the agenda," she offers. "But not on a murder case." "Yes, you're right," accepts Polly, pausing and cringing at how ridiculous she must have sounded. "But?" he asks, sensing her dissatisfaction. "But I feel I should be chasing something." "It's not your job." "You don't have my editors," Polly insists, knowing she isn't flattering his ego and could be offending him with the implication that they are tougher than his, not that she is necessarily implying they are better. "Even if I did, I wouldn't run around trying to do police work. Sometimes you just have to accept the trail has gone cold – as the bar man in Cognac said, it may never be solved." "And that doesn't bother you?" "It does, but I'm not sure I can do anything about it and there are greater injustices in the world." "I was hoping we might be able to do some digging together," ventures Polly, regretting as she says it that it sounds like the scenario of a bad Hollywood film with a sugary happy ending and the truth revealed to the wide world by a virtuous hero and heroine magnetically drawn to one another. "I'd heard de Massol was in Saudi Arabia and I'd love to know what he's finding out, wouldn't you?" she adds reaching for her glass for cover. "I'd be amazed if he can even stand the heat," says Pierre. "All the more reason for us to help him out with his enquiries," says Polly, with a forced smile. She no longer has any hope Pierre will take her seriously. The conversation moves on. How long has she been in Paris? Two years. Does she like it? Sort of. She feels unjustifiably glamourised by it, she declares, aware once again she is losing her interlocutor by saying something slightly weird. How long has he been there? Most of his life. Does he like it? Sort of. Can't say he feels glamourised by it, though. London would be sexier or even New York. "The grass is always greener on the other side – you say that in French?" questions Polly. "We say elsewhere, but yes, essentially. We're not so very different." Just cooler, thinks Polly and actually manages not to say it out loud. Instead she suggests another drink, but no, he has to go. First, he'll pay. With French gallantry, he insists this round is on him. Polly accepts, feeling fobbed off. He can give her a lift home, if she'd like. He's sure she can easily be on his way. She accepts, although it's obvious this is just a lift, and he leads her up the sloping, lop-sided street to his casually parked, not very clean car. Polly could never have slung her car on the side of a Paris street with such unconcern. She slides into the passenger seat and inches around a pair of high-heeled shoes abandoned at her feet. She doesn't ask to whom they could possibly belong.

12

Jean and Claudine Rivet are sitting down to dinner around a table that is far too big now their children are hardly ever there to join them. A fire crackles in the grate and still the room feels to Claudine to lack a heart. She has cooked skate with capers, white wine and cream and boiled potatoes, a staple of French cuisine she learnt to cook from her mother, who learnt from her mother, and she has served it countless times. In the days when they had promising, unlived lives ahead of them, Jean used to relish it as one of his favourite dishes. Now he barely notices what is on his plate. Instead, he is processing the frustrations of haggling over the price of *eau-de-vie* and debating how much, if anything, to tell his wife. On balance, the situation is not so critical that she needs to know how little the buyers are willing to pay and how he feels years of artisanal diligence have served only to leave him trapped on the periphery. Claudine for her part is fretting once again about Dominique and Thomas Fischer. She is uncomfortably aware that neither of her daughters has formed what she regards as a healthy relationship and that has to be in part her fault. It's a relief to both parents when the telephone rings. Almost comically, uneasy as lovers on a first date, they both leap to their feet and Claudine orders her husband to carry on eating. He is left alone with his skate while he hears his wife greeting their neighbour Simone with an enthusiastic *"Comment ca va?"* The reply is subdued and its sequel makes Claudine's fretting seem not so much prescient as to have actively evoked a negative reality, a potentially useful one, however, as she doesn't doubt for a minute that the information can finally break whatever spell Fischer has over her daughter. For now, she keeps it to herself. As she returns to the table, her husband shows no curiosity. His very bearing seems to forbid disclosure as he sits gloomy in front of his unfinished skate, locked into his cares.

Claudine is scraping uneaten food from the plates when Dominique strides into the kitchen, exuding nervous energy. Dominique has not turned up at home of her own volition for weeks. Her arrival paralyses Claudine with a mixture of amazement and the urge she knows she must stifle to pour out everything she has just heard. Experience tells her that abrupt revelations or enquiries would only drive her temperamental younger daughter, who cannot bear to defer to her parents on any point or admit her need for them, to take to her heels. "Are you hungry?" is all Claudine can think to ask. Dominique is not or if she is, she has decided not to admit it. She wanders into the dining room, kisses her pensive father on each cheek, helps herself to a glass of wine and heads for the stairs. "Hope it's okay if I stay for a day or two," she states over her shoulder. "I'm really tired now, but we'll talk in the morning."

13

De Massol is on his way to the university that al-Asad considered his legacy. Tasting the bitter unjust, unfreedom of a Saudi woman, he has a chaperone: he cannot be an unaccompanied man as he is visiting an all-women's university. Years after Oxbridge got rid of its single-sex colleges as an anachronism, in Saudi Arabia, female segregation offers the only prospect of allowing women into academia and De Massol supposes he should consider it a worthy legacy. He and his chaperone sit awkwardly in the back of another fiercely air-conditioned taxi that steers them through the city-scape of irrigated lawns and fountains and deposits them at a brand new intellectual metropolis. They are swept through electronic glass doors, then navigate the reluctant security and take a lift to an upper floor, then along corridor after corridor to an office again overlooking the shimmering Red Sea. The woman they meet is Dr Reem al-Wahida, a researcher with dark, almond-shaped eyes, circled with kohl. De Massol starts to offer his hand, then remembers any kind of touch is tantalisingly out of the question and hastily puts it instead to his pounding heart and bows slightly. He feels as if he is interviewing a timid, wild creature, who will flee to her lair at the slightest clumsy movement on his part. They begin therefore discussing her research. She is working on solar energy. The aim is to make it cheaper and overcome teething problems. Strange as it may seem, she explains, exposure to sun in the desert can be difficult as the panels become coated in sand and there is no water to wash them. But engineers can always find solutions and she thinks the oil men who criticise solar are misguided. It's helping to maximise Saudi oil exports and the revenues they bring in. Al-Asad understood that perfectly. Like her, he came from humble beginnings and had been educated with oil money. He wanted to ensure other people had that chance, even women. "Did anyone disagree with that view?" de Massol asks cautiously, himself, with an outsider's excess of reverence, ambivalent about disrupting the social hierarchy. "Of course," she replies. "Tell me all about him. What was he like?" de Massol says, almost lazily content to sit for hours on his hard, plastic chair, staring out at the shimmering Red Sea and occasionally, furtively, at Dr al-Wahida's huge kohl-circled, dark eyes, as absent of light as the sea is shot through with it. The desire to solve the case has become a remote, impossible aim. The quest for justice ebbs. As murders go, he tells himself, it was just a shooting. The victims were taken by surprise, but not tortured or terrorised in any sinister way, or so he assumes. The planet has merely lost three citizens slightly ahead of time and one of them had had most of the worldly success life could give him. His own job strikes him as being as futile as trying to investigate the killing of ants squashed beneath his heel. Dr. al-Wahida glances at the chaperone, almost theatrically, as if trying to make sure de Massol understands the parameters. With or without the protector of her honour, there are limits to what she can say and to what she knows. "The minister was very clever. He could have been an academic, but I think he liked the adrenaline of politics and world markets. He said he hated journalists though," she says. "Why?" "They snatched at his words. They took them out of context and made the markets move. He said they fueled speculation." "He didn't have to say anything, though," ventures de Massol, aware that he probably said too much at the first, perhaps last, major press conference of his career. "He said he had to give them something. They were so persistent." "And maybe sometimes it suited him if the market went up?" ventures de Massol. "He said not. He said volatility was always bad, though he said he knew plenty of people who were very grateful for it." The conversation meanders on. Dr al-Wahida is not saying anything de Massol couldn't have guessed, but he is struck by the impression of possessiveness. She is proud to be so familiar with al-Asad's thoughts. It could just be vanity or fantasy, but de Massol believes she has really spent hours and hours with the former minister. He is aware he cannot discover much about that now as the chaperone watches over them, so he deposits his card on the table and says he must return to his hotel.

Back in his room, de Massol is staring glumly at the gilt handles of the Barbie doll furniture, contemplating how quickly to give up and go home, when the mobile phone he has abandoned on a coffee table shudders with an incoming message. "There is something I forgot to tell you," Dr al-Wahida writes and daringly suggests they meet in an ice cream bar in the mall nearest his hotel. She doesn't mention chaperones. Neither does he, and, within the hour, the pair are eating ice cream accompanied with coffee, a combination de Massol would never have countenanced in France and yet maybe he will henceforth. In the absence of the chaperone, Dr. al-Wahida is less timid, de Massol more so as he wonders cravenly about religious police and the painful punishments they might find appropriate for foreign men consorting with unprotected Saudi women. "Is it safe to meet like this?" he ventures. "They won't create a scandal by arresting a visiting French policeman," Dr al-Wahida reassures him. "The only risk is mine." "So why are you taking it?" "I want justice. That man was willing to give me and other women like me a future." "So, what do you know?" asks de Massol, almost with a smile, not quite sure why he suddenly cuts to the chase, something he probably would not have done in his native French. In any case, he only manages to elicit another indirect answer. "I don't exactly know what I know. It's for you to decide if it's important," she says. They start again at the beginning. Dr al-Wahida met al-Asad when she was sixteen years old. He came to their school and wanted to meet the girls who were good at science. She was one. For her it was a magical, life-changing moment. He told her she would be one of the first scholarship students at his new university. When she went home to tell her parents, they told her not to get her hopes up. They didn't believe it. They didn't particularly want it to happen. It seemed disruptive. But she was determined. She still wants to make a difference. She doesn't want to just live another ordinary life that leaves everything just as it always was.

Al-Asad was good as his word and better. He continued to take an interest long after she got her university place. Once she had her degree and had embarked on research, he made sure she was invited to conferences and introduced her to the people from industry that needed her work, but, pre-empting de Massol's suspicions, she insists there was never anything improper about their relationship and he had helped other students, not just her.

Feeling further than ever from detecting any motives, de Massol orders more coffee and offers another round of ice cream, which is politely declined. "What I need," he says, thinking out loud rather than asking a question, "is a connection with the place where he was killed." "That is what I wanted to tell you," she replies. "My younger brother wanted to improve his English. The minister knew a teacher who had helped some of the ministry staff. He wasn't English. My brother never could quite work out where he was from. He thought his native language was German, but his English was perfect. I think he was an even better teacher because he knew exactly what it was like to have to learn the language." "And his name was Thomas Fischer," de Massol declares with sudden certainty. "That's right. How did you know?" De Massol brushes the question aside. "When did he leave Jeddah?" "In May last year. He said he had to get back to Europe and had some contacts in Cognac." De Massol is in shock and yet, he's not. Incredible as it is that Fischer should be connected to the Saudi oil ministry, he wouldn't put anything past him.

De Massol flags down a waiter for the bill and asks how Dr al-Wahida will get home. She says she has already arranged for her brother, the brother who perfected his English, to meet her. De Massol briefly contemplates interviewing him too, but a stomach made queasy again by the coffee and ice cream dictates it's time to head on his way. With a tinge of regret on his side, he takes one last look at the kohl-defined eyes, then Dr al-Wahida and they part to return to their respective worlds.

Once inside another air-conditioned taxi, de Massol calls his deputy Sébastien Tavet. "We need to question Fischer," he begins. "We're desperately trying to find him," Tavet tells him and says he was about to call. There have been developments, he says in a breathless rush. Castaniet has been found dead. He shot himself in his laboratory and would you believe it? Bénédicte Rivet was the first on the scene again. Two hours earlier, her mother had told the police Fischer and Castaniet were an item. She thought the police ought to know. Maybe it isn't just Saudi Arabia that has morality police. Fischer, meanwhile, has disappeared.

14

The coincidences are stacking up as in any detective story and as in the chaos of life, if you find time to notice. Bénédicte is numb. She had gone to Castaniet's lab. He was meant to be meeting some Chinese visitors and was uncharacteristically late to greet them. She was worried they would consider that a major offence and, as it was after noon, the time when his silent hours of tasting were over, she dared to knock on the door, which on a normal day would by then have been open. There was no reply. The door was locked. She knocked again and then she saw it, a trickle of blood flowing from beneath the door.

The emergency services duly arrived and forced their way in to find Castaniet with a gun in his hand, a bullet in his head and a flow of blood staining the pure white surfaces of the tasting laboratory. It has all the appearance of a suicide. No-one has discovered a note, but the gun he used was his father's pistol, handed down through the generations and now seeming to confirm that this is the action of a desperate son-less son. A nagging detail is that the window was open. It's a beautiful autumn day, but it is cold and Castaniet always preferred to do his tasting sealed off from anything but the taste and smell of the *eaux-de-vie* he was trying to blend. It's also remarkable that he chose a moment that amounts to a major breach of hospitality. Whatever his reservations about Chinese drinking habits, he was fastidious about decorum. But then again suicide always serves to remind us how unknowable other people are. Otherwise, unless we are murderers, wouldn't we have stopped it? Besides, he had been capable of slighting the Saudi minister.

Another of the coincidences is that Paul is in town again. He had arrived the day before Castaniet was found shot and had lured Bénédicte to spend a night with him. It's entirely plausible that he spent the morning in bed, though it's hardly an alibi, should he need one, as there are no witnesses. His car had stayed in the driveway beneath the linden trees and only Bénédicte had been seen leaving for work – confirmation at last of de Massol's jealous suspicions of a connection between them.

As she drove away up the single-track road, Bénédicte's mind had been a panic of conflicting emotions. The connection has strengthened. The previous evening surprised both of the wary lovers. Bénédicte found her interest growing despite her conviction that her first love for the unattainable Francois will always be her one true love. A part of her fears that love is only ever an unattainable ideal, dreamt up in medieval courtly society to disguise the socially-disruptive reality that knights only had time to rape and pillage, and that she wastes far too much time pining like the doomed maiden her sister thinks she is. Still, she's forced to admit Paul is not so bad. Paul also dropped his guard and let slip potentially incriminating information. She now knows that both he and Fischer have visited Saudi Arabia and more than that, met each other there. Paul said he had been on a trip to an oilfield, in fact not just any old oilfield but Ghawar, the world's biggest. He was taken there on some ridiculous PR stunt, as he saw it, designed to make everyone believe we could carry on relying on Saudi Arabia's giant reserves of light, easily accessible crude for decades to come, but having the opposite effect in his sceptical mind: if they were so confident, they would hold their peace and just get on with producing oil. Fischer, the anti-establishment environment warrior, had been there to help the oil world out with its English.

"But you behaved like total strangers," Bénédicte had objected, her mind flashing back to their sparring at Francois' party.

"We almost are," said Paul. "I didn't take to the guy. We'd

exchanged cards and that was about it. I'd pushed him out of my mind. I never expected to see him again and given his attitude towards me at that party, I didn't feel like mentioning our happy hours in the desert together."

Bénédicte's English is not good enough for her to put up a challenge or maybe she just had reached the point at which she wanted to give him the benefit of the doubt. After all, he had volunteered the information after she had poured out the havoc Fischer had wreaked in the Rivet household.

Now she finds herself again questioned by police about being first on the scene and Paul hauled in for good measure and then Dominique and her mother too. Cognac is incredulous, indignant, bristling with gossip, leaping self-righteously to unsubstantiated conclusions, while the police trawl for elusive evidence. Only Marie Castaniet, in dense quality, designer black, retains an icy, impenetrable calm. All she can tell de Massol is that she had no idea about Fischer and she has no idea where he has gone. She just requests the body will be quickly released, so she can arrange the funeral.

The Cauvet board is stung into another crisis meeting. The succession issue isn't as bad as it looks. They have a team of tasters and a real, chemical laboratory, concealed from public view, which establishes the science of the perfect blend. Irritatingly, however, the whole luxury branding myth of a *maître-de-chai*, whose perfectly attuned senses have been bred over the centuries, will have to be re-spun and then there's the issue of Fischer. No-one knows where he is or what secrets he possesses. That could be a problem. Furness declares in a tone closer to anger than his usual relaxed bluster that he will leave no stone unturned.

15

Ten days after the event, Thomas Fischer is roaming defiantly after a few drinks with Bernard Granger. Collar pulled up high, hat pulled down low just in case, he takes one last contemptuous look into the shop windows, full of designer luxury proudly arrayed, that line the silent streets. And just for the hell of it, in a premeditated, teenage-style prank, he tips a bottle of soap liquid into the fountain in Cognac's central square, turning it into an anarchic mass of bubbles beneath the full moon. He then wends his way along the wider, soulless streets that lead out from the centre to board the 5.20 a.m. train at the station next to the factory that makes the glass to bottle the cognac. Its giant chimneys belch out smoke like warm breath into the icy, clear air.

Fischer is far away, relishing the freedom of someone who only flirts with attachment to anyone or any place, when just over six hours later the bells begin tolling for

Castaniet's funeral, so he can be laid in the *terroir* to which he belongs.

Cognac's main church is wedged into one of the town's cobbled, pedestrianised streets, allowing no perspective on the Romanesque arch decorated with medieval angels and demons, frozen in a malevolent, amoral chase carved by anonymous craftsmen around the massive, central doors. The bells too seem designed for a much bigger space. De Massol feels as much as he hears their oppressive solemnity, resonating through his lean frame, and wonders whether anyone would attend his funeral. He shivers, telling himself it's the contrast between a cold, French November day and the recently-endured desert heat.

To bid *adieu* to Castaniet, all of Cognac's *beau monde* is present, along with the reluctantly tolerated press and the merely curious. The uncontested first lady of mourning is the improbably poised Madame Castaniet. The most poignant thing about her is the faithful Napoléon, who sits at her side as she greets the assembling congregation. Everything else about her forbids approach and above all questions. Napoléon is likely to reveal more than she. Polly cannot resist patting his black, velvet head as she slips past followed by Pierre and the rest of the visiting pack that has found new heat in a story that seemed to have gone cold.

The service, as everyone agrees, is perfectly judged. The coffin, made of the same Limousin oak as cognac barrels, is decked with lilies. Polly can barely take her eyes off it, fixated as she is by the thought it contains the body of a man almost as powerful in the Cognac world as al-Asad had been in oil. She's so fixated that she almost forgets that next to her is the man, full of life and passions she knows nothing about and is eager to explore, with whom she has travelled down from Paris, mostly in tense silence. In the row in front of them, is Francois with his aunt and cousin, then there are the Rivets, minus Dominique, and right at the front with Madame Castaniet are the remaining board members, the closest Madame Castaniet has to family apart from Napoléon. De Massol is at the back and a few of his team are carefully dotted around the church just in case there is anything to observe or anything to prevent. There is nothing obvious. Even Fischer's absence is hardly conspicuous. At the best of times, he would not have been welcome.

Respects elegantly paid, the journalists are discreetly led away to a press briefing on the future of Cauvet blending, arranged to distract them and allow those on the tightest deadlines to file their hasty despatches. The real guests are received at the Cauvet *château*, where on a summer evening Castaniet had deliberated over just how much to tell al-Asad about how the house of Cauvet buys its *eaux-de-vie*. De Massol is in this party. The police have been spared the journalists, officially on the grounds the verdict is suicide. De Massol doubts on various levels. Naturally, he doubts the verdict and in his paranoia, he fears the secret is out that press conferences are not his forte. In a desperate attempt to get warmer, he stands by the *château*'s blazing log fire and to his amazement Madame Castaniet comes over to him. Perhaps she too is just in search of warmth. Perhaps she too has no-one else to talk to beyond mere formality. "It was a beautiful service," de Massol begins. "Thank you," she replies. They could almost be talking about a wedding.

The journalists are in the Cauvet visitor centre in the room usually used to show tourists a film that unctuously relays the Cognac process from grape to glass. Special presentation decanters are displayed in glass cabinets at the back of the room. One, Polly remarks, is labelled "The *maître-de-chai*'s personal blend". "Wasn't it all his personal blend?" she whispers to Pierre, who merely shrugs.

Each journalist has been given a glossy paper carrier bag containing a Cauvet brochure and a miniature of Cauvet cognac, while Furness sets about trying to convince them there is nothing sinister about Castaniet's death and that the taste of Cauvet will outlive the *maître-de-chai*. The local press hears him out. The time-pressed visitors soon realise there is no real information to be had from a media-trained executive and so they make their excuses and wander out into the grey November day to scavenge elsewhere. The light is beginning to fade. The ANN man heads off looking suspiciously purposeful. Lelans tells them he's off to get a train, giving Polly her cue to make another play to win Pierre, hating herself once again even as she does so.

"Let's go and see the grave," she says.

"Why?" he asks.

"I don't know. I'm just curious. In the old days in Britain, you couldn't be buried in hallowed ground if you killed yourself. I don't think they're so strict anymore. After all, it would be harsh if they'd got the verdict wrong. It would be doubly unfair. First of all, you go and get yourself killed and then you get the blame for killing yourself."

"Castaniet will be in the family tomb. I'm sure of that and it's just a tomb."

"But it's sort of on the way," Polly coaxes. "It won't take long."

The cemetery is the main Cognac cemetery near the Rossignols' house and the Castaniet tomb is soon obvious for the opulent mass of flowers that stand out for being dazzlingly white. Everything else is a shade of drab. The tomb itself is of local limestone, grey and in places blackened. They say the blackening is a fungus created by the evaporating *eaux-de-vie*, the angels' share. Everyone in Cognac breathes it in all the time.

Gilles Louis-Marie Antoine Philippe Castaniet's name in clean, newly-carved letters has been added to the end of a long line of Castaniets dating all the way back to the eighteenth century.

"Just look at all those highly-respectable ancestors. Even if they're all dead and oblivious, he would have felt it his duty to continue. It must have been murder," muses Polly, aware that once again Pierre will accuse her of leaping to wild conclusions.

"Don't tell me," he says. "Madame Castaniet shot him in a jealous rage."

Neither is in the know about Fischer's potentially catalytic role. For now, the police, ever respectful of the establishment's need for discretion, sees no reason to disclose that and Polly in her infatuation and Pierre in his haste are too inattentive to notice that one of the wreaths has a card on it signed TF.

"If it were Madame Castaniet, it would have been perfectly controlled. Icy revenge," counters Polly, almost convincing herself. "But what if al-Asad's murderer is still around? Perhaps Castaniet had seen something and had to be silenced."

"You really have read too many Agatha Christies."

"Maybe. But you can't deny the fascination. Life is so rich and strange. We live it intensely and yet it hangs by a thread and someone can come along and snip it because of money or revenge or heart-break or ambition or some secret that the victim must never be allowed to utter. It's a fine line. You think only psychos would ever kill anyone, driven by compulsions that make all our passions and ambitions look feeble, but maybe it can happen almost by accident. Before you know it, you've snuffed someone out irreversibly without really meaning to and they have become just a handful of dust with no sense or feeling.

Once you've crossed the line, you can do it again and again. Maybe it will destroy your life too, but just maybe you'll get away with it and carry on unsuspected by the rest of the world and feeling entirely superior to the cowardly masses that muddle through never daring to do anything good or bad. We Brits, you know, are obsessed with whodunits. We like best the cosy ones that solve everything as neatly as a completed crossword puzzle."

"Well, we have Maigret," says Pierre, anxious to leave, not sharing Polly's tingling enjoyment of the gathering darkness and beginning to wonder just how bizarre this English woman is.

"Wasn't Simenon Belgian?" asks Polly.

"Maigret was French. Anyway, it's all fiction. This isn't. I've told you the guy in the Renaissance is right. They're never going to find the culprit and certainly not if they leave it to de Massol. He's not the man for the job. He's a small-town policeman and will be forever more. He just doesn't have what it takes to get to the bottom of this and I don't even get the sense anyone wants him to."

"That's what's so fascinating too," pursues Polly. "First of all, a completely random chain of events could have led to a murder, then it's random whether it will ever be solved. Even in this know-it-all age, we can't get to the bottom of every mystery. We can't know for sure when people are lying. We can't know what drives them and what they are thinking, though I've an idea you're not thinking too much of me."

"I'm thinking we should go and that solutions to supposed mysteries are often quite banal and disappointing. It's only the human love of fiction that dresses them up with meaning and metes out justice," says Pierre. And so, Polly again gets into his car. Again, she is sure the vibes are ambiguous at best and she is trying to force something that will never be and that she is too racked with self-doubt to defy any odds, but the pair of high heels is no longer on the floor at her feet.

WINTER

16

Francois is in his office staring at rows of figures. For the first time in his short and so-far stellar career, they appear as just that – figures, dull, boring, two-dimensional. He prefers not to ask himself why.

In the offices at the other end of the *couloir de la direction*, Bénédicte is staring at words and they too have no more than a superficial, transitory significance. Before her is one of the old publicity brochures. It contains a picture of Castaniet. He holds a glass of amber-coloured liquid, which he smells with his finely-tuned nose. Everything suggests harmony and pleasure. The sunlight glints on the crystal glass. His shirt is spotlessly white. His expensive cuffs are secured with cufflinks that Bénédicte notices for the first time are tiny Labradors, perhaps the one true love of his life, apparently crafted from gold. Next to the picture is a text in light grey on glossy white paper. It tells the story of the generations of master tasters, who select the finest *eaux-de-vie* and combine them into an exquisitely balanced blend from the various growing areas, the ones nearer the sea, which add just the subtlest notes of salt, and the rich, complex, mellow, long-aged *eaux-de-vie* from the sheltered vines deep in the Grande Champagne. To drink a great cognac, the implication is, is to become part of this noble tradition. To offer cognac to a friend is to share a privilege. All that is cruel, unfair and generally wrong with life is entirely forgotten. Only this golden moment of divine artistry exists.

Bénédicte's task is to write a new version, this time focusing on the science not the art. Intense brainstorming has concluded this is Cauvet's opportunity to shift the emphasis to twenty-first century laboratories that produce with precision a cognac to delight the senses. It will become a selling point. Whereas the other houses continue to rely on their human tasters, Cauvet has grasped the reality that modern methods create even greater blends.

Furness led the internal debate in his usual abrasive style, bustling on, with the implication that anyone who can't keep up with his thought processes is stupid. The absence of Castaniet means the absence of his severest critic. Even more than the Cauvets, it was he who was the defender of slow time, the insistent believer in considered thought and possessor of a reverence for tradition that Furness dismissed as cobwebby and uncritical. For Furness, it was driving with the brakes on. For Castaniet, it was watching a car crash.

Furness's rapid reasoning purposefully leaves no room for any nagging sentiment that Castaniet's demise has snatched away the soul of the company – or for tough questions on company profits. It's a matter of time before the world notices that Cauvet is no longer the number one, but Furness seeks to delay for as long as possible the vicious-circle, the self-fulfilling impact of lost confidence and allow more time for recent events to fade. In the absence of a swift resolution to de Massol's plodding investigation, he is counting on none. The last thing the house of Cauvet needs is for all the scandal to be revived when Furness hasn't given up on exploring the potential of the Middle East. The scandal wouldn't be so much the problem as the police scrutiny, though even that is a spur for the truly reckless who believe there is nothing better than a ban to make something more desirable. For them, no marketing strategy could be more enticing than the illicit lure of high degree alcohol under the brand of *sadiki*, the Arabic word for friend. A thirsty Saudi Arabian, Furness hears, is willing to pay hundreds of dollars for even the roughest, home-distilled *sadiki*. Offering an aristocratic alternative is an act of humanity.

The plodding de Massol for his part has been hauled before his boss. He is demanding to know what an expensive trip to Saudi Arabia has yielded. He is particularly unimpressed that during his absence someone potentially useful to the investigation decided to end it all, if indeed he did. Convinced he is about to be taken off the case, de Massol has barely the stamina to defend himself. The initial thrill that perhaps he could change his career for the better has given way to the shame-faced conviction he is doomed to fail. He merely lays out the pitiful sum of months of work. First the Rossignols and the distribution agreement, then the Fischer connection and then there's Paul Gray and Bénédicte Rivet, but Bénédicte is clearly innocent and Gray's crimes are probably unrelated. London regulators have been extremely unwilling to help a French-led enquiry.

Still, de Massol's mediocre luck hasn't quite run out. The show of displeasure is only a show. Unbeknownst to de Massol, his boss is more job-weary than he. Retirement is in sight. His performance and that of his underlings, barring an unprecedented catastrophe, will make no difference to his pension. Indeed, he can absolutely see the wisdom of not overzealously unearthing anything too disruptive. Ultimately, what purpose would that serve? He had been slightly worried he might have miscalculated with de Massol, but so far it seems his performance has been credible without being creditable. He can barely remember the days when he himself had higher motives, when he believed in purpose and change for the better and that he had a part to play. In his increasingly frequent idle moments, he occasionally wonders whether professional experience inevitably leads to the cynical belief that human nature is irredeemable and any justice subjective or is it just his professional experience that has corrupted him so completely? Maybe somewhere out there, there is a middle way between total cynicism and naive idealism that can leave vocation and integrity intact?

Fortunately for de Massol and his boss, the external drivers are as weak as their own consciences and wills. Al-Asad had no shareholders to clamour for profits to rise and expenses to fall and the social cries for justice are fainter by the day. Reem al-Wahida is very easy to ignore. The Saudis have a new man in the job. The markets have calmed down. The Cauvets have paid Mme Rossignol enough for her to start believing she must have imagined hearing anything about distribution agreements and Madame Castaniet is apparently living her elegant life as if Castaniet were never a part of it. Yet again, it seems, Bernard Granger is right: everyone will just heed the overwhelmingly strong urge to muddle on and the truth will never emerge for as long as it's left to the official channels.

17

Chez les Rivets, every dawn delivers a fresh stab of pain as Dominique awakes anew to the realisation that Fischer has gone for good. She has sufficient self-awareness to ask why it matters so much. Can't she be just as before? Is this actually just about wounded pride when now it's Bénédicte that's the loved-up sister and she's the jilted simpleton? Is it about failure, not heart-break? She was just a rebel making an adolescent point. She could choose a man and an identity that contradicted everything she was brought up to believe. Now she is forced to admit her parents' suspicions were founded. And yet somehow this is more than a delayed teenage identity crisis. She feels sapped. She sees no way forward. She cannot imagine choosing anyone other than the faithless Fischer. He has aged her before her time. There is a feeling of irreversible damage. Her mother too feels none of the relief she had fondly expected. Instead, a deep anxiety, if not foreboding, stifles the household as Jean Rivet broods in silence over the pitiful sums a great cognac house wants to pay for his hours and hours of patient labour so that their profit margins will surge and his will shrink. Of course, it's all relative, Cauvet's greed and Rivet's need. Rivet has a *maison bourgeoise* and a chunk of Cognac's finest growing area, which now holds the dubious honour of being the setting for an illustrious murder. The risk is, however, that all he surveys will soon belong to someone else. Claudine still knows almost nothing of the extent of his cares. She knows only that she treads a path between the quagmire moods of her youngest daughter and of her husband and is ever in danger of being sucked in. Bénédicte has been summoned to help. Just like old times, she is to go horse-riding with Dominique. It's the perfect day for a brisk gallop – clear and cold. Caspar and Oscar are ready and eager, snorting into the icy air, two brothers ready to bear two sisters. Bénédicte is dressed in the perfect riding kit. Dominique has her own self-consciously cool version minus a riding hat.

"You cannot not wear your hat," Bénédicte scolds. "It's freezing and it's dangerous."

Dominique just looks. Her whole attitude suggests refusal, like a horse before a water jump that it absolutely will not tackle.

"We can't go if you won't wear a hat," attempts Bénédicte.

"Then we won't go."

Bénédicte forces herself to stay calm. Dominique has a power to infuriate her that exceeds that of anyone else on the planet.

"It will be you who regrets it," she attempts to reason.

"Then it's my problem."

"And of everyone who loves you."

"Not many people do."

This is going nowhere, so either they are going nowhere or they are going with Dominique without a hat.

"*Bon bah... on y va,*" Bénédicte finally says and leaps on to Oscar.

Dominique follows and the two sisters are side by side, as they used to be, trotting off into the Grande Champagne. Soon they're at a gallop as the cold air spurs the horses on and Dominique, once again the fearless younger sister, snatches the lead as they head off towards the chapel of the Chevalier de la Croix Marron and the fields of bare wintry vines beyond. Ordering herself to live to the full this moment of continuity with the past, untouched by the anxiety of the relentless changes all around, Bénédicte repeats to herself like a mantra that Dominique never falls.

Paul is an only child. He did not have to compete for parental love. The *clou* lurking behind any relationship he forms and his capacity to inflict harm on his fellow human beings is the compounding effect of old-school public school, where any weakness had to be hidden beneath a carapace of arrogance lest it should be turned into a trigger for torture. He is at once guaranteed unconditional support and yet programmed to conceal tracts of his personality even from himself for fear of attack. He demands success and ignores obstacles, trying to understand them would be a waste of time. Better to move on, which on occasions involves getting very drunk.

Right now, he is back in his east London pad, ruefully serving coffee to Bart who has stayed the night because he missed the last train back to his Surrey suburb and his wife and one-year-old daughter. With Bart, Paul explores the best and worst sides of his character – the amoral frenzy to make a fast buck, the experimental consumption of absurd amounts of alcohol in defiance of physical damage and a blind loyalty to someone over whom he knows he has too much influence and yet cannot resist seeking to impress. He should never have let slip this crazy notion of selling alcohol to the Arabs. Bart has somehow become hooked in the absence of their other major Saudi trade.

Deep into their sixth pint when it still wasn't too late for Bart to do the right thing and head to the station and home, Paul had made the weakest attempt to reason.

"We're pushing our luck. We've earned enough. We can retire from this. It's not too late to become social workers."

"For me it was always too late," said Bart.

"You know I used to want to be a doctor," slurred Paul.

"It was that great crossroads moment. I was an idealistic seventeen year old about to spend my life selflessly dedicated to others for steady but not staggering reward. What could possibly be more worthwhile? But then, the school sent me on work experience. I spent a week in a hospital with a doctor who said all he did was prolong the agony. Ultimately, the outcome was always the same. He was sick of geriatrics who would never feel well again and breaking the news to unlucky thirty year olds and sometimes even teenagers that they probably had only months to live. They always wanted to know exactly how many and he said, you could never tell. That was the most consolation he could offer. He told me that doctors had the highest suicide rate of any profession. They have the means and they know precisely how grim life can be when all you can think of is pain, physical or emotional, that you can never move beyond. There is no point."

"Good job we're just dodgy dealers then with a fool-proof plan to make a lot of Arabs ecstatic," Bart had sniggered.

Then they'd drunkenly plotted until the small hours. Paul knew someone who was in the know, an old school contact. He'd get a tip-off ahead of the company results and they'd make squillions on the surprise profits delivered by an unlikely new market, not that the precise details could ever appear in a results statement. Briefly, they would be insanely happy.

Now in the clear light of day, they sip coffee and wrestle

with self-loathing as Paul's phone rings, or rather convulses with the boy-racer ring tone he has selected in one of his moments of poor judgement. Bénédicte's name flashes up and his entire bearing switches to an eager-to-please mode Bart has never witnessed.

"Ca va, ma chère?" he asks with a self-conscious glance at Bart.

"Ca va pas du tout," Bénédicte replies. "It's Dominique. She wouldn't listen to me. I knew it was stupid, but she never listens. She wouldn't wear a hat. She's fallen."

He pieces together the pieces that burst from Bénédicte. Does she want him to go over? She's not sure, but she doesn't entirely reject the idea. He takes that as a yes, sends Bart on his way and sets about organising tickets. At least he has some sort of plan for a day that risked disappearing in boredom, waves of nausea and a familiar nagging sensation.

De Massol, meanwhile, has been summoned by Madame Castaniet. To his astonishment, it is apparent she has been crying. It's not the crying, but the fact she has failed to conceal it that shocks him.

He follows her into her home. It's extremely elegant, but not quite a *château. Chez les* Rivets is in its way grander, but more run-down, more lived-in. With what is almost familiarity, Marie Castaniet leads him into the kitchen to offer him coffee. Her involvement in a domestic task in a domestic setting, like her tears, serves to make her less inscrutable. He suppresses an urge to put one of his long lean arms around her designer shoulders. Instead, he asks why she wanted to see him.

She does not directly answer, but he feels he will find out. For now, she just pours him coffee and pushes a sugar bowl towards him. He's sitting at a counter in the perfectly appointed kitchen where presumably Gilles Castaniet had sat a thousand times, although assailing his senses with coffee before cognac-blending was out of the question.

"I wouldn't have said Gilles was suicidal," she muses. "At least not more than anyone else. I mean, don't we all have those moments? Of course, we'd had our failures and humiliations, but he had a *raison d'être*. He hadn't lost the faith he'd always had. He believed it was worth doing things well, even if only for their own sake. He thought higher purposes could be left to take care of themselves."

"And Fischer?" de Massol dares to ask.

"It was all my fault," she says and the tears begin to well again, but it's quickly clear she is not talking about Fischer or her husband.

"I was out walking Napoléon and I let him off the lead. Everything happened so quickly. The Rivet sisters were out on their horses and somehow Napoléon ran into their path. Dominique's horse reared and threw her and Napoléon has run away. I've no idea where he is."

This is the most natural speech de Massol has ever heard Marie Castaniet make and he feels profoundly ill at ease.

"It couldn't have been your fault," is all he manages to say.

"I can't even control a dog," she sighs. "Or make a husband love me enough to bother to stay alive."

Aware of the still-glittering wedding ring, de Massol tentatively takes her hand. She does not withdraw it.

18

Paul knows that the first thing he should do is find Bénédicte – and yet he had a double motive for dashing across the Channel. And so, his path somehow takes him to the Renaissance bar and somehow Furness is there too. Paul can't work out what is driving him. Is it the need to follow through on a drunken pledge that he knows is an insane idea? He also knows the risk is that Furness just might help him, but only to trap him out of malice or expedience or both. It would be so convenient to believe in fate and to blame a higher stupidity than his personal fascination for doing the wrong thing.

"Well, fancy meeting you here," says Furness. They're off to a bad start. Both are on their guard.

Paul sits opposite him and orders a coffee from the hovering Bernard Granger, whose small, stodgy stature is made smaller by the height of the ceiling.

"Not drinking?" smirks Furness.

"I have to drive and I shouldn't stay long."

"But you wanted to see your old school chum?"

"I've been hoping to run into you. Seems a shame we should be strangers when I might be spending a lot more time in your neighbourhood."

"Oh?" enquires Furness.

"I've a few reasons to be here," says Paul, weighing how much he should reveal. The conversation would flow better with alcohol, but after his recent excesses, that's unthinkable. He considers he might even still be over the driving limit.

"Business? Pleasure? Don't tell me you're still helping the police with their enquiries?"

"Not as far as I know."

"But just in case, you've gone through your testimony very thoroughly with the charming Bénédicte Rivet?"

"Something like that."

"Then shouldn't you be rushing to her side? The whole town has already heard her sister's life is hanging by a thread."

Paul concedes he should. He also calculates that getting any commercial help from Clive Furness will require more than one attempt, and so he calls for the bill and strides off, but grinds to a halt on the cobbled street outside the minute he believes he is safely out of sight. In the broadest and narrowest sense, he is uncertain where he is going and has absolutely no idea whether this crazy plan can possibly materialise. He thinks back to the schemes he has pulled off and tries to recall whether he has felt like this before; whether he ever even paused for thought or wondered about the expanse of years possibly stretching ahead and whether he could carry on doing similar things over and over again and deriving the same sense of he knows not what. Satisfaction lasts a thoughtless second. After that, he is merely burdened with the realisation he cannot imagine how to do anything else and will only stop if someone forces him to. It's like breathing. The only alternative he can think of is not breathing.

For now, he is directionless. The hospital bedside is not his place. He sends Bénédicte a text to announce he has arrived in town and heads to the sanctuary of his Cognac home.

Furness lingers over his beer while Bernard Granger, picking up on the jagged vibes, hovers, hoping for a crumb to lend satisfaction to his never quite satisfying days.

"You two know each other then?" he ventures.

"Not really," Furness lies, or perhaps it's the underlying truth.

"He might be the culprit," suggests Granger.

"So might I. So might you. Does anyone even care anymore? Everyone's beginning to forget it even happened."

"Certainly, the police gave up weeks ago. Thomas Fischer

told me."

"You've seen him?" asks Furness, interest piqued.

"Not for weeks."

"But for fewer weeks than have passed since the police gave up?"

Outwitted, Granger hastily spots another customer to attend to. Furness shakes his head with theatrical knowingness and takes another sip of his beer.

19

While Paul Gray sinks into one of his leather armchairs beside a blazing fire, Tante Simone is sitting bolt upright at the kitchen table that has witnessed so much. She is making clear to Jeanne-Hélène and Francois her intention to go out into the raw winter's night and visit the Rivets as they keep vigil at a hospital bedside.

"I don't know whether they can face seeing anyone, but I can't just sit here. I must show them that I care. Someone from the village has to show their support," Simone declaims. Her motives are a tangle of conventional duty and the dark and strange. She feels responsible for setting in motion a train of events by passing on tittle-tattle that was in so many ways no concern of hers, except it had traumatised Jeanne-Hélène. She also knows what it is to feel cursed and to have a child the world regards as damaged. She could not swear that she does not somehow find solidarity – or it is *schadenfreude*? – in the thought she might have one less neighbour flaunting children's achievements and waving pictures of grandchildren. But equally, she has solidarity to give and equally she needs to be doing something other than feeling excruciatingly aware of someone else's unbearable pain. It's as if, even in the animated warmth of her kitchen, she can hear a death rattle.

"I should come too," says Francois, unexpectedly.

"No, you should stay with Jeanne-Hélène."

"Yes, yes," says Jeanne-Hélène, luxuriating in the increasingly rare prospect of an evening alone with her favourite cousin as Tante Simone leaves for a long, bleak drive to the main hospital at Bordeaux, fairly convinced she will hardly be welcome when she arrives.

"Let's make omelettes," says Jeanne-Hélène as soon as the door has closed behind Simone. Jeanne-Hélène loves omelettes and she especially loves Francois to make them for her. The "let's" is her way of imposing her iron will.

Her obliviousness is unfeeling; her zeal is callous, but there are many in the world who spend much of their time treating Jeanne-Hélène with dismissal. Reluctantly, Francois gets out the eggs and Jeanne-Hélène's favourite cheese and begins to beat with a vigour that takes him by surprise. Soon Jeanne-Hélène is busy eating, muttering repeatedly *"mais qu'est-ce que c'est bon!"* between mouthfuls, while Francois ruminates over whether to broach subjects likely to disrupt the mood. He probably would have refrained had not Jeanne-Hélène brought it on herself, as he would consider in hindsight.

"You don't make omelettes for anyone else, do you?" prods Jeanne-Hélène with her jealous sixth sense.

"Sometimes I do," says Francois, taking a very deliberate decision not to lie.

"For SSSSSophie," stammers Jeanne-Hélène.

"Yes, for Sophie," says Francois, attempting to clear away the plates, except Jeanne-Hélène grabs hers with a grip as iron as her will.

"Not fair," she says.

"Why not?" says Francois.

"You're *my* cousin."

"Yes, of course, but Sophie is going to be my wife."

The engagement is not yet official, but for the lovers it's certain. Francois is taking a foreign posting for Cauvet and the only way Sophie can easily accompany him is as his wife. He is paying Jeanne-Hélène the compliment of letting her be the first to know, but seen through her eyes, or even Bénédicte's, there is absolutely nothing fair about this English upstart snatching away in a hurried few months the region's finest youth. Sophie loves socially. It's all about image, status, getting a catch to make her the envy of her peers. Jeanne-Hélène loves with every molecule of her stammering being. She cannot articulate it beyond "not fair, not fair", but she knows Sophie and Francois will not make each other happy. It's not because Sophie is English and Francois is French, although that will be the generally accepted explanation. The reality is still simpler: mutual lust is only enough for nature. Their values are wildly different. In popular parlance, they don't get each other. Neither has realised the other has a completely different view of what the deal is. They will bask in glamour for a spell and then discontent will start to gnaw away. Once the foreign posting is over, Francois will have a strong homing instinct, while Sophie will declare it's her turn: they should live in England and she should have a career of her own, while Francois, bewildered and shocked, will argue they met on French soil and surely, she realised that, for him, being close to his family, given all it had been through, was at some point non-negotiable. He's also quite attached to philosophical conversations that wax into the small hours with a small group of friends that Sophie will come to find extraordinarily dull. If they have children, they will become horribly self-sufficient as they shut out the bitterness that taints the air. Then, at last, when the children are almost, but not quite grown-up enough, they will decide to divorce.

Jeanne-Hélène hurls the plate she had held so tightly on to the flagstone floor. One of her few advantages in life is that if she does not wish to conceal emotion, she feels no conventional obligation to do so.

"We want you to be our bridesmaid," Francois says in another heat-of-the-moment decision when he knows full well that it offers no consolation to his heart-broken cousin. There is none that he can offer. She runs off helter skelter to her room and he stoops to pick up the broken crockery from the floor.

When Tante Simone returns much, much later, she finds Jeanne-Hélène still awake and once again frantically praying. In Simone's morbid frame of mind, that seems totally appropriate. She kisses the top of her daughter's head absent-mindedly and collapses into bed.

20

Tante Simone had driven Bénédicte back not to her parents' home but to Paul's. Despite her fears, Simone had in a way been welcome at the stricken bedside. Certainly, she was useful. She had persuaded the hospital to give Dominique's agonised parents, who refused to leave, somewhere to sleep, while Bénédicte, obviously desperate to escape, had begged her to drive her away and blushingly admitted she wanted to stay with the Englishman Paul Gray.

Bénédicte has always found comfort in Tante Simone and she especially draws comfort from her on this long, cold journey. Tante Simone endures. The tragic scars have been softened by time. The very fact of her continued existence implies that extreme pain can be overcome, even if life is never as promising again. She is too fatalistic, though, for Bénédicte's taste. From experience, she instantly assumes the worst because hope is too traumatic. Bénédicte hasn't reached the point when she can allow herself to believe that the sister with whom she has so many unresolved conflicts might never give her benediction. That would be an irreversible triumph for Dominique.

Worn down by emotion and exhaustion, Bénédicte finds herself telling Tante Simone what she assumes she knows. As she stares ahead into the night, she recounts that she is unrequited by Francois and has thrown herself into the arms of an Englishman she cannot fathom. She ranks herself among the countless millions to have failed in the pursuit of true love and to be cynically considering a lesser alternative. Really, she says, in the bleakness of her mood when everything is only of relative importance, it's no big deal. Love is just an indulgence. Is it even real? Surely, it's just civilisation's gloss on an instinctive urge that lasts just long enough to ensure reproduction? She feels guilty at the confession, half thought, half spoken, when she should be thinking of nothing but Dominique. Still it's easier to confess when Tante Simone's eyes are fixed on the almost empty motorway ahead, like a priest neutral behind his screen, and she says almost nothing in response. While the rest of the world sleeps in dull routine, Bénédicte's revelations are dream-like and yet she will wake up and they will be true. She feels her words give indelible reality to emotions that might have faded away, never articulated. She tells Tante Simone about the first time she saw Paul, when he had been completely unsure what to do, and then at the chapel and finding Jeanne-Hélène, when he scooped her up and marched her home. "That was the night when everyone had seemed to be in a state of high passion," she says, trailing off, thinking of Sophie and Francois and finding the pain of the memory almost as acute as re-living the moment of Dominique's fall. That seems unreal, impossible. Sophie and Francois' togetherness fills her with an overwhelming sense of inevitability.

But Paul is nearly enough. He shakes hands with Tante Simone, almost like a French man not an embarrassed English man, and invites her in for a drink, perhaps something warm on a cold night? But no, she must get home and leave the lovers huddled together; Bénédicte entirely vulnerable and Paul allowing the carapace of invulnerability to fall away.

It's as if one half of Cognac is taking refuge in each other's arms, while the other is just in despair.

De Massol, in thrall to Madame Castaniet, has spent the day hunting for Napoléon. They began where the fall happened. They searched the ruined chapel and found autumn leaves, dead flies and the smell of earth mingled with dank stone. They scoured the hard, cold ground around and the only clue it yields to the dramas played out there is a Labrador cufflink. Madame Castaniet picks it up and convulses with an unearthly, dry sob, while de Massol looks on, at a loss as to whether her emotion is for the memory of the man who used to wear it or the dog that inspired it. Maybe both.

De Massol has the sensation of being locked in a moment from which he will never emerge. He sees himself and Madame Castaniet as two figures in a painting, viewed from on high to make them appear particularly small and lost as they go round and round in circles, propelled by some exterior force of malignity or stupidity or utter indifference as flakes of snow begin to fall, rare indeed in Cognac.

Chilled to the bone, they repair to the village restaurant and order steaming pots of *mouclade* with crusty bread. De Massol is hardly a gastronome, but he finds this *charentais* and, to him, superior version of *moules marinières* deeply comforting and he realises he is starving. By Madame Castaniet's restrained standards, so is she. They order extra bread and, recklessly, a second glass of wine.

Madame la restaurateuse is thrilled by the enjoyment of her elegant guests. She tells them the recipe was her grandmother's and chit-chats about the weather, enough to make anyone hungry, she supposes, even someone as refined as Madame Castaniet.

"We've spent the day looking for my dog," offers Madame Castaniet, adding to pre-empt the question: "We haven't found him."

The *restaurateuse* is suitably moved and offers to put up a picture in case someone has seen him. She wants the details, though Madame Castaniet is certain she is already well-informed. When was he seen last? A day ago. Where? Near the chapel of the Chevalier de la Croix Marron. "Ah, the place where the accident was?" she asks in a whisper of exaggerated sympathy. Yes. Madame Castaniet does not venture that Napoléon was the cause for fear of drawing the enmity of the village upon him, though again she suspects the local gossips knew before she did.

"I don't like to be nosy, but in fact he was your husband's dog?" the *restaurateuse* asks as she scoops up the clattering *mouclade* pots.

"He was always mine too," murmurs Madame Castaniet, stung to be denied even the warmth of a first claim on the affections of a dog.

"It's just I wondered if he might be at the grave. I've heard it's something dogs do. Somehow, they know. Maybe it's the scent that attracts them."

"It's hardly likely through all that stone," de Massol intervenes if only because he feels he should be part of the conversation.

"But it is possible Gilles had walked him there," says Madame Castaniet. "After all, it is the family tomb. Gilles visited it and I took Napoléon there at the funeral. I'm certain he knew."

Suddenly the warmth of the *mouclade* and the ongoing current of daily life are slipping from reach. De Massol reconciles himself to a trip to a cemetery on a winter's night as the snow begins to thicken. They travel nervously, nervous at what they might find and not find, nervous as they peer out through the swirling snow, anxious about the cold Napoléon must be feeling and horribly aware of the coldness and loneliness of a tomb. De Massol is also aware of the Rossignols' house and is thankful the shutters are firmly shut, meaning Madame Rossignol cannot be looking out at the car of a policeman who has failed to deliver justice. They enter the cemetery, leaving tracks in otherwise unsullied snow lying about a centimetre deep.

De Massol is mildly surprised to see the wreaths from the funeral are still at the tomb – as is Napoléon, looking more velvety-black than ever as he whimpers at his master's grave. "Were you scared my darling?" Mme Castaniet murmurs, throwing her arms around Napoléon and nestling her face against his noble head with a tenderness de Massol cannot believe her husband ever enjoyed. He seizes on her distraction to scour what is left of the wreaths, wondering why they are still there, all dead and dusted with snow as if no-one but Napoléon has visited the tomb, not even the police, he admits, reproaching himself. Stealthily, he gathers up the name cards, bleached by rain and now damp with snow, but perhaps still just about readable, and then offers to drive Madame Castaniet home with her cold, hungry dog.

21

In essence, de Massol and Mme Castaniet are as similar as Sophie and Francois are different. They have fought for the position in society Sophie and Francois had as a birthright and that matters enormously to Sophie and not a jot to Francois. They cannot attain Francois' insouciance, but they have been forced into confrontation with life beyond appearances.

While Madame Castaniet sleeps through her preoccupations and Napoléon dreams in his basket in a corner of the perfect kitchen restored to his perfect canine ability to avoid questioning comfortable surroundings, de Massol is poring over the cards he has rescued from the desiccated wreaths. It would take a forensic expert to retrieve most of the heart-felt sentiments, but some have survived the ravages of the weather, perhaps because they were more sheltered, perhaps, he thinks fancifully, because the feelings were stronger, at least when compared to all the other socially appropriate, dutiful attempts to soothe in the face of the bleakest of realities. Madame Castaniet wrote: "Forever in my thoughts, Marie." She has the good taste to be credible, he thinks, whereas "Always faithful" would already be a lie and in any case more appropriate to Napoléon. TF, as Polly and Pierre entirely failed to notice, simply wrote TF. The most interesting thing was that this overt despiser of convention wrote anything at all, but the real surprise is Clive Furness: "I owe you a great deal." What did he mean? Is this English irony? Yet again de Massol has the sensation he is puzzling not over clues, but over random fragments, striving for a coherent narrative from what might be no more than a brief eruption of professional rivalry. Can he suspend his disbelief sufficiently to dig in and maybe get his own career back on track? He attempts again to piece together the little he knows. The world's then most powerful oil minister was found riddled with bullets, as were his wife and a driver, who happened to know about a plan to sell alcohol in the Middle East that could have made him just as much as al-Asad the target. Sometime later, Castaniet, also one assumes in the know, has also been shot, perhaps by his own hand and Thomas Fischer, the obvious link between the two, is missing. So far, an international arrest warrant has yielded nothing and de Massol feels a curious lack of pressure to deliver any results in a case that he had assumed was career-defining.

As an extension of the words and gossip that glue society together, journalism's task is to deliver narrative meaning, a manageable semblance of truth. Polly's problem is her abundance of self-doubt. She reproaches herself for a lack of vision when she sees the bold statements others make, whereas an ounce more arrogance would make her dismissive of all sweeping generalisations that are not her own. The ANN man, otherwise known as David Alvarez, has trained himself to be only strategic. In the friendless bubble he inhabits, he knows nothing of moral dilemmas. He is in tune with the times. Self-doubt is not useful. Professional integrity is optional. Journalism is perfect for him. He can look on as a sanctioned observer without ever intervening to do the right thing, licensed not to feel the kind of sentimental sympathy that could be mistaken for bias. The main aim is to invest his energies in the most efficient possible – read intellectually and morally laziest – way to make an impact. He need only know just enough to communicate to the widest readership. He hasn't even bothered to learn the language of the country he for now inhabits. English is nearly always enough to extract the bare minimum he requires. Any more would slow him down. Approaching the Christmas news lull, with no intention of heading to the States on leave, he is casting around for a story he can push to its prize-winning limits and when he looks back over the year's crop, he thinks the strange events of Cognac might just about serve. There are all sorts of threads to tug at – police incompetence, Saudi in-fighting and he's sure that one of France's finest luxury products can yield a wealth of dirty secrets, past and present, if only one looks. Without it even flashing through his brain that he should seek permission or any debilitating recognition that colleagues might have higher claims, he books a train ticket and a room in the Renaissance. It also doesn't occur to him to take a cameraman with him. That can wait until the recce is over, he thinks.

22

Blessed with a self-believer's luck, David Alvarez's timing could not be better, although the lack of a cameraman is an error.

His train pulls into the sleepy Cognac station beside the glass foundry needed for all those Cauvet bottles and he walks on to the small forecourt, where he confidently expects the car he has ordered will be waiting for him. It isn't. He would be ready to curse an entire continent and its stubborn insistence on putting quality of life ahead of raw capitalism and customer service, except his journalistic instincts are pricking with the sense his driver has a tolerable excuse. It's the smell that alerts him. It's the smell of the evaporating cognac intensified and mixed with smoke and when he looks towards the town, he sees an apocalyptic glow on the horizon. Magnetically drawn, he begins walking towards it, with his laptop bag slung over his shoulder and his wheelie suitcase rattling over the cobbled streets behind him. The houses are silent. The shutters, tightly shut, their natural defensive state, and the traffic as absent as in the middle of the night. He walks through the main square and the bars are empty. He arrives at the Renaissance. It too is dark and empty but for a lone receptionist waiting specifically for him, the only customer. She stands behind a shabby reception desk lit by a lamp that has the air of being borrowed from her grandmother's bedside. In her broken English, she tells him what he has already sensed: the warehouses are on fire. Virtually everyone in the town is helping to douse the flames. She will help later, as soon as Monsieur Granger returns. Alvarez almost flings his suitcase at her for safe keeping, calls the office and shouts out orders in a manner that brooks no questions, and heads for the river.

Everyone who is not already there is walking towards it, with the exception of one furtive figure who registers on his trained consciousness as perhaps an important detail, but for now Alvarez must follow the crowd. The mood is primeval. Individuals are horror-struck, but collectively there is feverish excitement. This is the moment everyone has dreaded and for which everyone has for years prepared. Now it seems inevitable. The Cauvet fire brigade has mobilised a public desperate to be part of the action. A human chain, stretching along the bank, over the bridge and to the blazing warehouses, is handing along buckets of river water as enthusiastically as if it were a party game.

The effort is destined to be futile. If the professionals with their engines cannot extinguish the flames, it is already too late. Decades of ageing *eaux-de-vie* have been claimed prematurely by the angels and the earthly *paradis* guarded behind bars in revered glass demi-johns is no more. Alvarez is already shaping a script in his head as he records video footage on his phone. He feels big statements are entirely justified. This is no minor setback. This is the death of a great French luxury brand, a symbol of the arrogant, the deep-rooted, the long-term collapsing before the march of aggressive, quick-thinking, U.S.-led fast-buck-making. Alvarez wouldn't of course put it quite like that, joyful as he is to witness the demise of something that, for all its faults, is implicitly a criticism of his ignoble *modus operandi*. Very soon, before the markets open and start dumping Cauvet shares, he'll have to craft a few hard and objective-sounding, yet compassionate words, but for now even he is mesmerised by the spectacle. This must be the end of Cauvet and with it, the way of life of a community bound to it for centuries, however misguidedly. All the crooked intelligence and desperate strategy of Furness and his ilk cannot turn this around. The years of careful marketing to weave the myth of cognac as a social, almost necessary good, and to gloss over the dirty tricks, cosy nepotism, affairs with secretaries, ripping off of *viticulteurs* and damaging of livers are undone in a night. A cognac house is nothing without its stocks. At the very least, the proudest of the cognac houses will have to merge with another and a few very rich people will become slightly poorer. At worst, the not very rich will become very poor.

SPRING

23

Birds are singing in the empty burnt-out warehouses. Their songs are loud and energetic as they build the nests to breed the singers of future years. Weeds wrap themselves around devastated timbers left in an unrepaired, un-demolished suspension pending the insurers' final decision, although everyone knows no pay-out could make good the loss. Polly meanders through the ruins, thinking melodramatically of the ruins of her career. David Alvarez roundly scooped her. There is no official point her being here. She's here on her own dime, something Alvarez would have never done, but she needed to find a way to put all the *actes manqués* behind her. She thought interviewing a few other failures hoping to rise from the ashes just might help with what she sees in her exaggerated gloom as the complex, overwhelming, exhausting task of pulling herself together. She toyed with the idea of persuading Pierre to accompany her, but she has at last decided the only dignified route is to leave him for the owner of the high heels. She doesn't even have the catharsis of heart-break; there is no emotional legitimacy in mourning a relationship that never was. So here she is alone, busy envying the chirruping sparrows their purposeful industry, telling herself she's once again in the wrong place at the wrong time when she catches sight of Jeanne-Hélène. She remembers her vaguely from that party she had to leave for another wild goose chase. It had registered on her consciousness that something was amiss with Jeanne-Hélène but she couldn't have said precisely what. Now it is obvious Jeanne-Hélène is not what the world calls normal. She is on her knees and praying to some higher authority. There's nothing casual or half-hearted. Her entire being is devoted to the task in hand. Polly is torn between the belief the most delicate thing would be to leave and a fascination that holds her there until a hidden rhythm to which only Jeanne-Hélène responds makes her finish her ecstatic devotions and look Polly straight in the eye. *"Je suis desolée,"* says Polly, uttering in French a very English sentiment considering she has done nothing wrong. *"Faut pas,"* says Jeanne-Hélène. *"Pas ta faute. Ma faute, ma faute, mamamama ffffaute."* "What's your fault?" asks Polly, gently. Normally, she would be hurried. She would have no patience to talk to someone so unlikely to yield useful information quickly, but today she feels no pressure. After all, she's here on her own dime and it's curiously liberating. Could it possibly be that the entire system of employment contracts is an entirely distorting incentive? "I did it," says Jeanne-Hélène, gesturing at the burnt-out warehouses. "Really?" asks Polly, incredulous. "But why?" "Wasn't fair. Nothing was fair." "Life isn't always fair," says Polly, wondering if she is just humouring Jeanne-Hélène or witnessing a full-scale confession. She doesn't know Jeanne-Hélène well enough to realise that she feels no compulsion to accept what convention makes the rest of the world condone. "Let's go and get some coffee," says Polly. "I think we need to talk about this." *"Tisane,"* pleads Jeanne-Hélène. "Ok, *tisane*. It's true, it's much better."

They talk on and off for hours in the back room of one of Cognac's two tea shops. It's a week-day afternoon and the place is empty but for the waitress who supplies them with a steady stream of boiling water to replenish the linden flowers, dried from a summer ago. Jeanne-Hélène's stammer forces Polly to concentrate intently to decipher meaning, to weigh every word and wonder how true it is. The total is a jumble of connections and the connections are Jeanne-Hélène's connections, requiring knowledge Polly is aware she doesn't always have. They begin with the fire. How did she do it? Matches. Cognac burns. How did she get past the security? Easy, no-one would suspect her. She doesn't count. Then they work backwards. Why? Wasn't fair. Nothing was fair. Needed Francois not to leave. Needed Monsieur Rivet's *eaux-de-vie* to be worth lots of money. Didn't like. What didn't she like? Didn't like nasty Cauvets. Didn't like English girl. Not fair.

After seemingly hours of "not fairs", even in her leisure Polly decides it's time to leave. But what about Jeanne-Hélène? Jeanne-Hélène says she's fine. She knows how to get home. Polly wrestles with her conscience. She feels she should take her there or perhaps to the police, but what would they do with a confession like this. Polly believes it, but she's not sure anyone else will and if they do, would their malign sense of justice see a purpose in measuring Jeanne-Hélène by society's unimaginative standards? Polly could of course write about it. Finally, she has her scoop and yet ironically, she thinks, this is better police work or social work than journalism. Journalism resides in some half-way place between the tawdry and the heroic. Her editors would doubt it all. They'd worry about legality. They'd never take it from Polly. "Can I at least get you a taxi?" asks Polly. "Bus stop," says Jeanne-Hélène. So, Polly pays for the *tisane* and they walk through the sleepy streets. Polly is forced to slow from her usual pace to accompany Jeanne-Hélène's awkward gait. It's not quite a limp, but for Jeanne-Hélène the effort of walking like everything else is more keenly felt than by the mass of humanity. They pass the Renaissance to the main square and the bus-stop to wait for the bus that heads out to Grande Champagne. Polly resolves she will go there tomorrow, but for now she contents herself with seeing Jeanne-Hélène safely on to public transport. "Goodbye," says Polly, feeling a tug at the heart strings as Jeanne-Hélène struggles up what she makes seem steps for giants. Jeanne-Hélène turns with an after-thought: "Thomas told me to," she says as the bus doors close. "He told me it wasn't fair." Polly has no doubt she means Thomas Fischer, well able to imagine that he would have used Jeanne-Hélène without a second thought.

24

Bénédicte is sitting in a pub in London, watching Paul standing at the bar, tall and straight and waiting to be served. She is seeing him for the first time in his own element, almost as mysteriously other as another species. She has a flashback to seeing the startled deer she nearly killed a life-time ago, or so it seems, and then to the startled Paul she first met, lost and bewildered on her territory. Now he is at ease, understanding without even considering there is something to understand or not understand in all the codes that puzzle her. Dazed as she is, she feels a thrill of ownership that he is showing her his *milieu*, alien as it is. Beside her is his friend Bart and at the next table is the kind of group typical in London but amazing to Bénédicte for a raw, unthinking sense of entitlement that assaults her fragile senses. It's a group of thirty-something women, eagerly serving each other from a bottle of wine delivered with a cooler – needless given the speed they are drinking.

While Bénédicte nurses her secret pain, they chatter and laugh and outdo each other with tales of expensive travel to exotic spas and yoga holidays and men, in and out of favour. To Bénédicte, they all look alike with their highlighted hair and high-street office fashion. "Which one would you choose?" she asks Bart, genuinely curious. "None of them. I'd choose you," he says gallantly. He likes this woman. He likes that she just says the slightly odd things on her mind and maybe, in some corner of his mind, he reluctantly welcomes in a premonition that Paul's dangerous days could be behind him. Bénédicte smiles wanly. It's far too soon for her to emerge from her guilt-stricken grief. Paul insisted on this trip for a change of scene. She said she could not leave her parents, so he appealed to them and they agreed with him in their selfless concern that their one remaining daughter has a life to live. They've even started to like this smooth English man so different from Dominique's fatal choice and now he's at Bénédicte's side with pints for him and Bart and fizzy water for her. "Not drinking?" asks Bart. No, she isn't. "She doesn't really," she says, stifling any insinuations. "Growing up with Cognac somehow put me off." Her sobriety sobers all three of them and Bart is soon excusing himself for the commute home to his wife and child, who will welcome the influence of Paul's new-found decency, while Paul and Bénédicte walk along the river bank towards his flat. They walk in silence, Paul for fear of saying the wrong thing and Bénédicte because she's wondering if this is the moment she should speak, beneath a moonless sky, beside the mighty Thames, inky-black and chilling and lapping as if a salivating beast ready to snatch anything into its jaws. "I have to tell you something," she begins, feeling how little she knows this man and how unable she is to gauge his reactions. "Of course," he says, absent-mindedly, almost accustomed to the string of high seriousness that has replaced his frivolous trading days. "I'm pregnant," Bénédicte whispers. Paul stops in his tracks, grabs her and looks intently into the big brown eyes that look fearfully, tearfully back, then he clasps her to him and she murmurs into his high-quality coat sleeve. "I have to keep it. Whatever it is, I have to call it Dominique."

25

Jean and Claudine Rivet are sitting round their too-big table with Tante Simone. As the village elder in grief, Simone has arrived with a pot of soup for her stricken neighbours, believing it's just about the only substance they could swallow. She's laid the table for them and opened wine in a doomed attempt at heartiness.

For the Rivets, there are instants when they still believe the door will open and Dominique will burst in from another room where she has been hiding all the time in one of her sulks, but then there are hours and hours when they are oppressed by the knowledge that all the electricity that held together the intense personality of Dominique has gone to earth.

"I just hope Bénédicte will forgive herself," murmurs Claudine. "She says she should never have allowed Dominique to ride."

It's a mantra Claudine has uttered daily and her husband

delivers his customary, patient response as the soup is served.

"No-one could stop Dominique doing what she wanted to do," he says, thinking he is beginning to get used to the past tense and that too horrifies him as if the grief is less raw, the wound healing and the memories of that vivid face and so-often furious voice beginning to blur.

Between such fragments of conversation and pauses heavy with thought, they sip their soup until the telephone rings. Claudine takes the call. It's Bénédicte with the one piece of news that can offer any kind of consolation to an ageing mother who has just lost a child. She was going to wait to tell them in person, but Paul thought she should tell them immediately. He thought they would want to know now. Simone tells them he's right. This is a wonderful sign. There is hope. There is new life. "You can be happy again," Simone declares, even as she dwells on the bitter knowledge she will never have such happiness because neither will Jeanne-Hélène – wherever she is, she suddenly thinks, realising she has not seen her for hours.

"I must go, but you know I'm there for you. I'll call by soon," she says and takes her leave to seek out her daughter.

Jeanne-Hélène is content enough. She is back from her wanderings and her praying to discover Francois is in residence. She finds him sitting at the kitchen table staring into space, something she has never seen him do before. "What's wrong?" she stammers. "What's right?" he asks, thinking even Jeanne-Hélène cannot be impervious to a tragic accident and a devastating fire on top of murder and suicide. "But there's something new?" Jeanne-Hélène persists, instinctively homing in on any development important in her scheme of things. "Something's happened to you." Francois sighs. He's loath to tell her what he knows will delight her; that one earthly paradise the fire destroyed once and for all was his with Sophie.

Once it would have thrilled Bénédicte too to know the man she has spent so much time desiring is free, but now, she would prefer ignorance. She must focus on this relationship forged *in extremis* being the right choice if indeed she really had a choice when who else would take on someone so damaged and guilt-ridden and with a graciousness she had never anticipated? They could be better suited, she could be more fulfilled, she could be generally a lot luckier, but ultimately, would she feel so very different once the raw agonies of grief have subsided?

Francois feels as if the flames have consumed his entire future, not just his foreign assignment and with that his plans to marry Sophie. He is struggling to not think of the family curse he associates with this place. He came to break the cycle – and perhaps he has. The clarity of his realisation that his love for Sophie was only as strong as a job offer told him he had to end it now. But what does he have instead? His career is reduced to staring at depressing figures that increasingly fail to add up in an office that used to smell of the angels' share and now smells of smoke.

26

In Jeddah, a throng of men in perfectly laundered white robes flows into a gleaming conference centre. The image of immaculate white in the intense Middle Eastern light is dreamlike and yet ostensibly the assembly has gathered to discuss what could be a prosaic essay question in a dreary examination hall: "the re-evaluation of fossil fuel in the context of renewable energy".

High on the podium, learned doctors, engineers and representatives of the oil ministry are aligned around one empty seat, reserved for the new oil minister, while international businessmen and academics sit in the audience, nursing their mobile phones and laptops like children given toys for a long journey. Dr Reem al-Wahida is huddled at the back in black with a handful of other women and the press corps. There are a half a dozen foreign correspondents, who have travelled down from Riyadh, local press and reporters from industry publications. They could struggle to find news, even from the oil minister. He is no longer quite so brand new that any syllable would be enough to excite an editor. The best might be a useful business card grabbed from someone in a break for coffee and dates or for prayer, definitely not prayer Jeanne-Hélène ecstatic style. The general tenor of the conference is empty insincerity. The content of the speeches has been vetted to ensure they reveal nothing at all. Any Q+A on a subject that strikes to the heart of a kingdom that has risen from Bedouin poverty to concentrated wealth will also be deadened by assiduous rehearsal. To complete the pretence, the non-content will be dutifully translated into English or from English into Arabic if the speakers are foreign – and who should be in the interpreting booth but Thomas Fischer? Interpreting is a task that suits him perfectly right now and he is exceptionally good at it should he ever decide to pursue an honest career. It requires his full concentration, but little thought and no feeling. He is a superior machine, hearing one language and cynically spitting out another. He knows about Dominique. Furness has told him. Furness was transparently eager to impart the news or rather to witness Fischer's reaction. Fischer revealed nothing more than mild surprise. It wasn't part of his plan, but it doesn't change anything. Bénédicte is now the sole heiress to the Rivet property, whose *eaux-de-vie* have surged in value. He supposes that one day Jeanne-Hélène is technically entitled to the neighbouring estate, also now worth far more than before the buyers' ability to dictate the price was spectacularly destroyed. He relishes the chaos, but he had never really cared about any of that. Sabotage is for him a purer motive than direct gain. Gain is Furness' end and that has left him with angry Saudis on his back, denied their distribution agreement. For now, all he has is smuggled *sadiki* and a not unreasonable dread of being found dead in a sandy ditch unless he resumes contact with his old school rival Paul Gray, who is well on the way to taking on the Rivet property, Fischer surmises. Even Fischer is not hell-bent on inflicting more pain on the Rivets, but the burgeoning happiness of the arrogant Englishman, who seems to be denied nothing he wants, is a tempting target.

Reem has spotted Fischer. She has dozens of questions to ask him, but without her brother, she can see no way to make any kind of approach without causing a scandal in this tip-toeing-on-eggshells, if you're a woman, society. Her months of deft, meticulous research into her brother's language teacher have revealed depressingly little. She's not even totally sure where he comes from. Her brother was vague. Wherever it was, it was somewhere far and European with dense forests and harsh winters – maybe Luxembourg, maybe Switzerland, maybe Liechtenstein, possibly Austria. She has tried discreetly to extract a few facts from the ministry. She knows that although he did some work for al-Asad's people, he was brought in by those loyal to the new man. He then went to Cognac and seems to have had several meetings with Cauvet board members named Castaniet and Furness. And now here he is, apparently on good terms with the new régime, which is just entering the room to take up the empty podium seat. The room falls silent. The mobile phones and laptops are briefly laid aside and the proceedings officially begin. Reem is barely listening. She's pondering her suspicions that Fischer was sent off to Cognac to eliminate a minister no longer popular in some quarters for shifting the balance away from oil. They thought he was being utterly selfish. They considered him an old man who had made his career and now was changing the rules for everyone who might follow so that they could never attain the power and wealth he had enjoyed. They were too stupid to see that al-Asad's vision was more lasting and strategic. Today's renewable conference would have him turning in his grave as nothing more than lip-service for the benefit of the outside world. There is not a shred of evidence, but her theory strikes her as possible, indeed likely. Cognac, with almost no security and every chance a crime could take place entirely free of witnesses, was an ideal setting. But it's also obvious that the Saudi police will never touch Fischer if he is as close to the ministry as she suspects. As the speeches drone on, she searches out de Massol's number and texts him that Fischer is here, sitting in an interpreting booth.

De Massol would have cared passionately when he was

still locked in what seems now a naive conviction there could be glory in solving this crime. Now his phone is buzzing unattended. Too content to have any drive, he sits in the Renaissance bar with *une pression* before him staring at the television. It's showing his favourite of the Franco-Belgian spring classics: the Paris-Roubaix, which takes a cycling élite over the punishing cobbles of an area that used to hum with mining industry. Now that industry is long dead, the trauma of its passing is a faint collective memory and Roubaix is just a nondescript frontier kind of place but for this annual moment legendary among cyclists for its pain.

De Massol finds himself briefly envious of their crazy endeavour. It's in a sense pointless and yet its definition of success or failure, at least to an outsider, is straightforward, even heroic. He has of course utterly failed to make any difference.

The Paris-Roubaix fascinates Paul too as a symbol of aspiration and defeat. Even now, as he twists self-consciously the gleaming new wedding ring that announces the hasty marriage rural French society has required, he is filled with the sense that he has yet to fulfil his potential honestly in any sphere. He stares at the television screen and is thrown back to that day not even a year ago that has changed his life and he finds himself scouring his memory as if he has lost something that he can find if only he can retrace his exact mental steps. He remembers the overwhelming heat, the silence, the shattered glass, Bénédicte, the child and now he remembers there was something else too: a black Labrador just like the one sitting patiently beside de Massol as he sips his lager.

For all Bénédicte's prudish dislike of gossip as the life-blood of so small a town, she has told him about Madame Castaniet and Napoléon's new master. Of course, it may not have been Napoléon that he saw, or it may have been just Napoléon, but it may just be that Castaniet had been there too. If only dogs could talk. Paul's wrestles half-heartedly with his conscience and weighs up the relative peace of his days and his instinctive dislike of de Massol. In any case, is there any point telling him about a possible witness that is even less useful than the three-year daughter? He finishes his *pression*, pays Granger and heads off to his harmonious, centuries-old *Cognacais* home and to Bénédicte, who is no longer quite so *petite*.

Epilogue

Three years later Polly is back in London, bored and dissatisfied. She has switched from correspondent to copy-editing, which has shortened her working hours but robbed her of any engagement in the story. Whereas she used to leave the office in central Paris at almost any hour and wander home through streets lined with Haussmann apartment blocks to her tiny but central flat, fifth floor *sans ascenseur,* much of her energy now is consumed by the trudge in up the crowded Northern Line from a conversion in Balham she's renting until she has a better plan. For much of her working day, she is focused consciously or unconsciously on how to leave the office at an hour that will make the commute home as painless as possible. Once a vocation, the work has become a chore. She's just one of the less vital stages in the hit-and-miss process of seeking truth and trying to order it, while senior management obsesses over what kind of information can make the most money. Polly happens to be staring at an oil market report

– "Market rises on fears of supply disruption" – when the phone at her desk rings. It's the switchboard. Will she take a call from someone who doesn't want to give her name? In a previous, busier life, Polly would have said no, but now she welcomes any disruption.

The mystery caller is willing to tell Polly she is Dr. Reem al-Wahida from Jeddah. She has been reading stories Polly wrote about Cognac and the late al-Asad and she thinks it would be useful to meet. She is in London. She's come here to attend a conference. Polly is intrigued. They exchange mobile phone numbers and fix a *rendez-vous* at seven o'clock at Brown's hotel in Mayfair, where Polly is impressed to discover Dr. Al-Wahida is staying.

After digging out all she can on Dr. Al-Wahida from the web, Polly is the first to arrive. She sits in a deep armchair in a corner of the wood-panelled lounge where she can almost forget that Brown's, like everywhere else, has been taken over by an international chain that could struggle to preserve its timeless Englishness. In any case, Polly reminds herself tradition for tradition's sake is not a good thing, but she can't help but think of Miss Marple noticing something subtle had changed about Brown's and that, like every other detail her beady eyes observed, it was relevant to solving the puzzle at hand.

While Polly is slightly early, Reem is on time. She has daringly shed her *abaya* and is impeccably neat in a navy trouser suit and a matching headscarf. She establishes Polly is Polly with a swift phone text and heads to Polly's corner of the room with alacrity. They order tea even though that is possibly not what either of them really wishes to drink and then they cut to the chase.

"So why did you want to talk to me? Not the ANN man or the French press or perhaps you already have?" asks Polly, thinking wistfully of Pierre.

"I read your article about Cognac after the fire. I sensed you knew more than you were saying. With the men, they said more than they knew," Reem says with a sly smile.

Polly is won over, disarmed and impressed. Reem is soft-spoken, outwardly unforceful and yet strong. She has sought her out and is here alone in London, a highly-educated Saudi woman, something of an authority on renewable energy, who speaks English with barely a trace of an accent. Desperate for an adventure and finding more reasons to trust Reem than not, Polly almost launches into her story of Jeanne-Hélène there and then, but she is after all a journalist. She is meant to extract information first, so she asks what Reem knows.

Reem's trump card is that she has met al-Asad's daughter, who is back in Saudi Arabia and living with al-Asad's first wife, and who now, three years on, seems to remember something about her early life trauma. From what they can reconstruct, there were two attackers, both men, and Reem thinks they were Castaniet and Fischer. It's even possible al-Asad's daughter would recognise his killers.

"I'd bet on Fischer, but I'm not sure about Castaniet," says Polly and she tells her all about Jeanne-Hélène.

"We need to talk to Jeanne-Hélène again," says Reem.

"We could try," says Polly, but she's not convinced. She can see Reem wants justice for her beloved oil minister and despite the rush of warmth she feels towards her, she's wary of any Saudi justice that might break Jeanne-Hélène as well as the more truly guilty. Once a believer in justice for its own sake, something she instinctively strove for, even Polly can see it can become subjective.

"Tell me again why you think it was Castaniet and Fischer," she asks to win some thinking time. Reem is suddenly fluent, almost loquacious.

"Fischer is an anarchist. He cares for no-one. He's willing to work for anyone if it means inflicting damage on a society he seems to despise. He got hired by those in the ministry who wanted to get rid of al-Asad and either he or they decided that Cognac was the place to do it. In any case, he found some reason to go there and started pushing his way into the local society. He met Dominique and opportunistically started an affair with her. He also met Castaniet and Furness and he played them off against each other. Furness was trying to do deals in Saudi and Castaniet hated that. Somehow Fischer made Castaniet obsessed with him. Castaniet gave him all the details of al-Asad's visit and together they got rid of him and his wife and driver too. Then Castaniet found out Fischer was still working with Furness and they had a furious row that ended with an apparent suicide. Fischer left the country but not before persuading Jeanne-Hélène to finish off his destruction of the house of Cauvet."

Polly is stunned. It's plausible. It's not so far from what she thought, but she's pretty sure Reem has no proof.

"I know what you're thinking," says Reem as Polly sits sipping her Orange Pekoe.

"That it's a great story but I could never print it because we have absolutely no evidence," she replies. "And if we went to the police, they'd laugh at us."

"That's where you come in," says Reem. "You have to help me find some proof." For a complicit moment, it feels like a manageable challenge. They promise to stay in touch. They exchange cards. Reem tells Polly she expects her to visit Jeddah and Polly tells Reem she must return to London and then she heads out into the London night, down into the Underground and a pleasantly uncrowded post-rush-hour commute to what for now is home.

FIN

ABOUT THE AUTHOR

Barbara Lewis is a journalist whose career has taken her to London, Hong Kong, Paris, Brussels … and Cognac. She read English at Jesus College, Oxford, before setting out as a trainee reporter on the Bromsgrove Messenger, where she covered anything from golden weddings to murder to the arts. A passion to explore the world beyond Britain led her to leave local journalism for international news agencies, currently Reuters. Another passion is theatre and she wrote a sell-out play for the Edinburgh Festival. This is her first novel.

36014849R00116

Printed in Great Britain
by Amazon